Gilda

(Original title: The House that Guilda Drew)

by RICHARD PARKER

Cover by

John Fernie

SCHOLASTIC BOOK SERVICES

NEW YORK • TORONTO • LONDON • AUCKLAND • SYDNEY • TOKYO

Copyright © 1963 by Richard Parker. This edition is published by Scholastic Book Services, a division of Scholastic Magazines, Inc., by arrangement with The Bobbs-Merrill Company, Inc., publishers of the book under the title THE HOUSE THAT GUILDA DREW.

3rd printing .... March 1973

Printed in the U.S.A.

Contents

The Ant Taxi

GILDA WATCHED her mother unpacking the groceries she had just bought at the supermarket. "Did you get any bacon?" she said.

"Of course I got bacon."

"Good," said Gilda. She lifted the mosquito netting that curtained the opening of the tent and draped it over her head; the whole world turned green.

"Don't do that," said Mrs. Ronkoop. "How many times I have to tell you?"

"It's interesting," Gilda said. "Everything is prettier."

They were camped at the side of a shallow, muddy lake and it was February, summer. The camping ground was a hard-baked clay patch. The few clumps of grass here and there at the feet of the gum trees were dead and brown. The gum trees themselves were a dull grayish green. The water of the lake was brown. No wonder everything looked prettier through the mosquito netting.

Mrs. Ronkoop looked up and said suddenly, "Why are you so interested in bacon, anyway? I thought you didn't like it!"

Gilda had folded and folded the netting and now held a thick bandage over her eyes; she couldn't see anything at all, not even her mother advancing across the tent toward her. The slap on the arm made her jump so much that when she snatched the netting away from her face she tore her fingers through it.

"Now see what you've done?" said Mrs. Ronkoop angrily. "I said you'd tear it."

"Oh, you didn't!" said Gilda. The tears in her eyes were more of anger at her mother's injustice than pain from the slap. "And, anyway, you tore it more than I did."

Mrs. Ronkoop was very hot and tired after walking back from town along the dusty road in the blazing afternoon sun. She wanted to go down to the toilet block and have a shower. Also her ankles were beginning to swell, as they did in summer. She said, "Don't give me any cheek, you Gilda. Get the needle and sew up those holes you made or we'll be eaten up tonight by the mosquitoes."

Gilda stamped across the tent, thinking

to herself how little noise you could make with bare feet on the earth floor, and opened her mother's needlework box — a cardboard box that had once held tins of peaches. But instead of looking for the needle and thread she watched her mother return to the task of taking out the groceries.

"That's it," she said suddenly. "That's the bacon!"

"I know it's the bacon," said Mrs. Ronkoop sharply. "What *is* the matter with you? Bacon, bacon, bacon!"

"I want the bag it's in," said Gilda. "The lady at the supermarket always slips it into the bag without creasing it up, so it's good to draw pictures on."

"Is that all?" Mrs. Ronkoop was sorry about losing her temper. "Here you are then. Go away somewhere and draw your picture."

"What about the mosquito netting?"

"Oh, I'll see to that when I've had a shower. Go on! Go on and draw."

Gilda knew that this was her mother's way of saying she was sorry, so she smiled and took the crisp brown bag. She went through to the back half of the tent where the three beds were and pulled her own private box from under her camp bed.

Gilda's private box was a wooden one, an apricot case in fact, with a piece of hardboard for a lid and rope right round it to hold everything in place. She was not allowed to have more private possessions than would fit into this box. Moving from place to place the way they did, there just wasn't room for more.

From her box she took a tin of colored pencils and using the lid of the box to rest on she began to draw on one side of the bag. She drew a house.

It was a white clapboard house, one story high with a red roof. At the front there was a wide veranda with a decorated rail and climbing vines up its sides. She put a very modern carport at the side of the house but no car in it, because the car they had was very old and battered and rather ugly, and she wasn't sure what sort of a car she would have liked to have. In fact she didn't care much about a car at all, except of course you had to have one. What she cared about most was the house.

Gilda could not remember at all clearly what it was like to live in a house. Her parents had brought her to Australia when she was six and now she was eleven and a half. At first they had spent nine or ten months in a reception center and she vaguely remem-

8

bered that as being rather horrid. They had lived in two small rooms in a long corrugated iron building. Gilda could remember hearing the babies of the other families crying at night. She had cried herself sometimes.

Since then they had always lived in a tent. Her father traveled around working at different kinds of jobs; seasonal work they called it. Just now he was at the canning factory putting peaches in cans. But once all the peaches at that place had been picked and canned there would be no more work in Shepparton and they would move on somewhere else.

She gave her house bright blue curtains, and a curly iron front gate with a yellow letter box beside it. Then she tried to make the lawn look very smooth and very green. You'd have to water it every single day to have a lawn like that, she thought, but it would be worth it.

She drew herself sitting on the veranda with two friends. They weren't doing anything; just gloriously sitting in those comfortable veranda chairs that have backs and arms and a jutting-out piece in front to put your legs up on.

The Ronkoops had camp stools but no armchairs, because there wouldn't have been room for them in the trailer. You either had to sit up to the table on a camp stool or lie on your bed; there was nothing in between.

When she had finished her picture Gilda put it away with the pencils into her box, roped the lid back on and put the box back under her bed. Then she sat on her bed for a moment wondering what to do next. It was really too hot to do anything energetic. She would have liked a swim, but the lake was too shallow and muddy and the swimming pool was almost a mile away on the other side of the lake.

At that moment there was a distant scream which Gilda recognized as the four o'clock train, so she went out of the tent to watch it go past. She waved to the driver who waved back as usual and then she counted the trucks. There were sixty-four and eight of them were double-decker sheep trucks. The smell from them was very strong after the train had passed.

A flock of about twenty huge white birds with black faces and long black beaks were disturbed by the train, although they must have been quite as used to it as Gilda was. They flew up out of the marsh on the far side of the track and circled around the cannery building before settling back out of sight again.

"Just an excuse to make a fuss," said Gilda, speaking aloud to herself.

She thought she might get a piece of steak from the icebox and catch some crayfish for tea, but catching crayfish by yourself isn't much fun. Instead she got a few crumbs of cake from the cake tin and dropped them in one of the ants' roadways that wound back and forth across the camp site. Almost immediately the crumbs were picked up by large ants that began the long journey back to the colony up on the railway embankment. Gilda bent down to watch them and slowly followed to see that they got their burdens safely home.

They were sugar ants, about a half an inch long and black except for the tail part which was dull red or sometimes purple. Gilda didn't mind them because they didn't smell and they hardly ever climbed up your legs. They didn't bite either unless you actually sat on them, and you could hardly blame them for that.

Gilda kept her eye on the ant that was carrying the largest crumb, and followed slowly. It crossed the bare clay of the camping area, falling down cracks now and then and butting itself against bits of tree bark and dead leaves but never losing its piece of cake. Every now and then it stopped and got a fresh grip of the cake crumb before hurrying on again.

"Why are you in such a hurry?" Gilda asked it. "Why don't you sit down for a minute and take a rest? Would somebody growl at you if you did?"

Come to think of it she had never seen an ant taking life easily. Surely there must be a few lazy ants. There were certainly clever ones and stupid ones. This one was not very bright; it seemed to fall over everything.

"You shouldn't have taken the biggest piece," Gilda said. "You can't even see round it. That's why you keep bumping into things."

Between the campsite and the road there was a narrow strip of wiry brown grass. It must have been like thick jungle to the ant. It scrambled up grass stems, fell off them, got caught among the roots, all in a desperate hurry but never letting go of the piece of cake. Soon it was quite lost and was going in the wrong direction.

"You're going right out of your way," Gilda told it, but the ant took no notice.

She put her foot in the way, trying to

turn it, but the ant climbed straight over and carried on.

"Oh, really," she said. "You must be the silliest ant that ever lived. I bet the others let you carry the biggest piece on purpose. They're probably laughing like anything behind your back."

The ant was now heading back the way it had come. Gilda felt quite fond of it for being so simple. She put her hand down on the ground in front of the ant and when it started to climb over her she raised her hand up.

"Now, just sit still," she said, "and I'll take you right to your front door."

The ant kept dashing on and would have walked straight off into the air if she hadn't put her other hand in the way in time. She had to keep changing hands to stop it pitching off the edge. She crossed the road and carefully approached the fence at the bottom of the railway embankment.

"What are you doing?" called her mother who had just come back from the shower.

Gilda saw her out of the corner of her eye, but did not dare to look up from her hands. "I'm running a taxi service for ants," she said.

"Such crazy," said Mrs. Ronkoop.

The ant suddenly stopped rushing, put down its burden and began to polish up its legs and its antennae. The cake crumb rolled off Gilda's hand and disappeared into the grass.

"Oh really!" exclaimed Gilda.

The ant didn't seem to care. He bent an antenna over just like a branch of a tree that you've pulled down to pick peaches off. Then he dashed to the edge of Gilda's hand and straight off into space just as if the air was solid.

"Gilda!" called Mrs. Ronkoop. "When you're finished, come and help me with the tea, yes?"

Old Bomb

WHEN HER FATHER came back from work they all spoke in Dutch together. Gilda didn't really care for this because she found English much easier to speak and often forgot the Dutch word for something, or else made mistakes and was corrected by her parents. They never corrected her English because she spoke it better than they did.

"They are putting men off now," Mr. Ronkoop said. "Not much work left. Today only eleven tons of peaches came in. Most of the orchards are cleared."

Mrs. Ronkoop was pleased. Of all the places they had camped in, Shepparton was the most uncomfortable. "When shall we go?" she asked.

"Tomorrow or the next day," said Mr. Ronkoop.

"To Mildura?"

Mildura was the center of the vineyards,

and the grape-picking usually started sometime in February.

"Good," said Gilda. "Then we shall see
Ronnie and Robyn."

"Probably," said Mr. Ronkoop.

"Why probably? We always see them at
Mildura. Every year you and Mr. Brunt
work together on the grapes."

"Yes," said Mr. Ronkoop. "Every year so
far. But nothing is arranged. Maybe one
year Brunt gets a good job somewhere he
doesn't want to leave. Maybe some time the
Brunts get a house and settle down in one
place."

Gilda looked closely at her father's face
to see if he was serious. It was hard to tell.
Mr. Ronkoop had a broad, almost flat, face,
and one of his eyes was gray all over as the
result of an accident. This meant half of his
face didn't have much expression, and that
was the half that was turned toward Gilda.

"Don't tease the child," said Mrs. Ronkoop. "You know how much she looks forward to meeting her friends each year."

"I'm not teasing," Mr. Ronkoop objected.
"Well, not much, anyway. One of these years
we shall not meet the Brunts at Mildura.
Maybe this year."

"One year," said Mrs. Ronkoop. "But *not*
this year. I have a letter. I almost forgot."

She searched in her pocket and in her bag, but the letter was not in either. "Never mind," she said. "I read it and they are going to Mildura and will be there on the twelfth of February."

Gilda began to search on the floor of the tent and even in the icebox. "Do you think you could have dropped it in the showers?" she said.

"Do you think I read letters in the showers?" said Mrs. Ronkoop, and laughed. "Such crazy!" The last two words she said in English; it was a favorite expression of hers and she would not be convinced that it was wrong. All the same Gilda was determined to find the letter as she thought it might have a message for her. And in the end she found it in the bottom of the box Mrs. Ronkoop had carried the groceries in. The letter started off "Dear Coopie," which was Mrs. Brunt's name for Mrs. Ronkoop.

"Can I read it?" Gilda asked.

"If you like."

The letter was not long and did not say much more than Mrs. Ronkoop had already said. But at the end was the sentence Gilda was looking for. "Tell Gilda, Ronnie says, they have put him into the sixth grade at last. Seems a pity to move again, but we'll be up at Mildura all right, don't worry."

"There," said Gilda. "You didn't say about Ronnie getting into the sixth grade."

Mrs. Ronkoop shrugged her shoulders. "He will be back in fourth grade again at Mildura," she said. "You know how it is at the school there."

And this of course was true. One of the chief troubles for children moving around was that they never settled into a school long enough to learn anything. Half a term here and half a term there, and the teachers could hardly be blamed for not taking too much notice of pupils who were not going to stay in the area. Gilda had been in fourth grade for three years now.

"I wish we could live in a house like other people," Gilda said.

Mr. Ronkoop grunted. Then he lit one of the stubby little cigars he always smoked after tea and went through to the back half of the tent and lay down on his bed to read the newspaper.

Mrs. Ronkoop shook her head warningly at Gilda to show her that her father was offended at what she had just said.

"But why?" said Gilda, suddenly feeling stubborn and awkward. "If other people do, why can't we? We're not different really."

Her mother began to clear the table and made a shushing noise at Gilda.

"You always say 'shush' but you never explain," said Gilda loudly. She knew this was not quite true, but she said it just the same.

Mr. Ronkoop's voice came from behind. "There is such a thing as money."

"You get lots of money," said Gilda brightly. "I've seen it at the end of the week when you give Mother some."

"Yes, lots of money," he growled. "And from this you eat well and have new clothes when you want them. But a house eats money. A house is a great hungry monster. If you were in a house you would be often hungry and often wear old and ragged clothes. What is the use of a house if you must be poor to live in it?"

"I don't believe it," said Gilda.

Mr. Ronkoop snorted and shook out his newspaper with an irritated snap. "You have long to live and much to learn," he said. "But, anyway, as you are so interested I'll tell you. I've saved a little money and one day maybe it will be enough to buy a house with. Now that is enough about houses. Finish!"

Gilda knew from the tone of her father's voice that he really meant what he said. All the same she wasn't entirely satisfied and whispered to her mother, "How much has he saved?"

Mrs. Ronkoop glanced over her shoulder and then held up eight fingers.

"Eight dollars?"

"Eight hundred."

"Eight hundred!" exclaimed Gilda, forgetting to whisper. "I should think you could buy a beautiful house for that much."

"Well, you couldn't," came her father's voice. "Eight hundred would only just about buy a plot of land to put a house on. And now be quiet both of you."

Gilda sat out in front of the tent watching the sun go down for a while. The white birds with black faces and beaks — called straw-necked ibises — flew up and perched in the bare branches of a dead tree. All the ants went away as they did each night at sunset, and half a dozen kookaburra birds came shouting and laughing like noisy children into the trees above her head. Then the mosquitos rose from the marsh beyond the railway line and descended on the campsite and Gilda retreated hurriedly, scratching her bare arms, within the safety of the netting.

The evenings were the worst time. Now and then they went down to the café at the gasoline station and watched television, but that meant buying a supper and was too expensive to do very often. In any case Mr.

Ronkoop was asleep, and from the way he was snoring he did not seem likely to wake up for hours.

Gilda pulled her box out from under her bed but pushed it back again without even undoing the rope. She got the insect spray and sprayed a little around the tent in case any mosquitos were hiding in corners, and then she sat down on her bed and sighed. About ten minutes later she sighed again and went to bed.

Mrs. Ronkoop thought to herself, "Poor Gilda. She is a lonely one. Never mind, she will be happy again when we meet the Brunts."

The following day Mr. Ronkoop came back soon after midday. "All finished at the canneries," he said. "Only the permanent staff now. Everybody else finished."

"Can we go then?" asked Gilda.

"Tomorrow morning. We'll make an early start," he said. "Tonight we go to the café and have two suppers each and watch television all the evening."

And so they did, though they did not actually have two suppers each but one supper and then a milk shake and a slice of fruit cake later, and an ice cream later still. They watched three television programs, one after the other, and Gilda fell asleep during the third with her arms on the table and her head on her arms, so that she had to be wakened up to walk back to the tent.

The following morning they were all up at five before the sun rose, and they were eating their breakfast when the kookaburras had their morning laugh in the lakeside gum trees. Packing up was a very scientific business as each box and case and roll of bedding had its special place in the trailer. They had done it all so many times, however, that the whole packing took only half an hour, and there they were with all their worldly possessions either on the trailer or in the back of the battered old car.

Gilda sat between her parents on the front seat and tried to keep her long bony legs out of the way of the gear shift. And they drove and drove and drove for hour after hour through the flat brown countryside. Miles and miles and miles, and each mile so much like the one before that Gilda dozed and sometimes wondered if they were really going anywhere at all. Every hour or so they passed through a town and Mr. Ronkoop said the name of it as if to prove that they were getting somewhere and not merely going round in a circle.

After five hours' driving they stopped to stretch their legs and eat some sandwiches.

Mr. Ronkoop lit a fire by the roadside and boiled a billy so that they could have a drink of tea. Then he stretched himself out in a piece of shade and went to sleep. Gilda wandered along the road to where the white rails of the bridge were visible about a quarter of a mile away. The creek that should have run under the bridge had dried up, but there were one or two pools in its twisting bed, so she took her clothes off and lay down in the deepest one. The water just covered her and was like warm tea. When she felt something wriggle under her she jumped out, and when the sun had dried her again she put her clothes on. It didn't make her any cooler, but it did make her feel cleaner and more awake.

When she got back to the car her father was awake and ready to go on. They drove for two more hours and then, right in the middle of nowhere, the car stopped.

"Gasoline?" said Mrs. Ronkoop.

Mr. Ronkoop looked at the gauge and shook his head. "Plenty," he said.

He got out and opened the hood. He thrust his arms in and turned this and twisted that and got black grease up to his elbows. Then he wiped the sweat off his face with his forearm and put black grease on his wide flat face. After about half an hour Mrs.

Ronkoop and Gilda got out of the car and sat in the shade of a tree. A little later Mrs. Ronkoop made some tea and found a packet of cookies. By this time it was about four o'clock and not quite so hot.

Every now and then Mr. Ronkoop would get back into the car. They would hear the whirr of the starter join in with the whirring chorus of the cicadas on the trees, but the engine would not start.

At about five o'clock Mr. Ronkoop kicked the front wheel viciously and said something in strong Dutch. Then he put his head in the engine and the hood fell down and hit him on the back of the head.

He dragged himself out and kicked the other front wheel.

"Old bomb!" he said.

A House With a Tower

W HEN IT was quite obvious that the car
could not be persuaded to start, the Ronkoops pushed it and the trailer off the road
and prepared to camp for the night. The
verge was a strip of flat ground twenty or
thirty yards wide, so that in fact it was not
a bad place to camp, except of course that
there was no water and no power. But they
had a five-gallon water carrier and could
perfectly well cook over a fire.

Mr. Ronkoop studied the sky and decided
not to go to all the trouble of putting up the
tent. It would mean less unpacking and less
packing up again the following morning.

"Only necessary things to come off," he
said, and scientifically unloaded the beds,
bedding rolls, food boxes, dishes, and cut-
lery. Then he unloaded the five-gallon wa-
ter-carrier and walked back to the camp
swinging it and whistling.

"Now what?" said Mrs. Ronkoop. Mr. Ronkoop never whistled unless he was upset.

He set the water carrier down on the ground. "So!" he said, and hit the side of it with his fist. It gave off a hollow note like a drum.

"I must have forgotten to fill it before we left," said Gilda. This was her job. She picked up the carrier and looked around. "I'll go and see if I can find some water now," she said. "There's bound to be a house somewhere."

"Oh yes," said her father. "Bound to be. You can see one, perhaps?"

Gilda looked on all sides and the bare brown paddocks stretched in all directions as far as she could see. Not a roof anywhere. "Well, perhaps I'll find a creek," she said. "Anyway, I'll find *something*. It's my job."

Mr. Ronkoop took the carrier from her and put it back in the trailer. "So!" he said. "There is a little water in the water bag; that will have to do until tomorrow. But another time, please to remember."

Gilda felt absolutely dreadful. There was nothing her father liked more at the end of a tiring day than his large mug brimful of boiling hot black coffee. There couldn't be enough water left in the water bag for more than a couple of mouthfuls each.

At that moment a car came along the road, the first they had seen since their car had stopped. It slowed down and drew into the side by them. A thin-faced tanned man put his head out of the window.

"Are you all right?" he said.

Mr. Ronkoop waved his hands disgustedly at the battered car dragged in disgrace on to the verge. "That old bomb," he said, "she let us down."

"Anything I can do?"

"Oh please, yes. At the next garage you come to," said Mr. Ronkoop, going over to the car and explaining how he would like a breakdown truck sent out in the morning to give them a tow.

While he was talking Gilda went to the back of the trailer and took out the water carrier again. Then she hurried away, dodging between the trees at the side of the road and hoping to be out of sight by the time her father was free to look for her again. She was determined to make up for her mistake somehow or other.

When Mr. Ronkoop had finished with the man in the car he went back to his wife.

"I heard you," she said. "Such crazy."

"How crazy?" he said. "She doesn't go, does she? We cannot stay here for the rest of our lives."

"But such expense!"

Mr. Ronkoop drew the corners of his mouth down and raised his eyes to the heavens. "Don't talk about it," he said, "or I shan't sleep all night. Tomorrow will be soon enough. Where is Gilda?"

"Getting wood for the fire, I think. I saw her through the trees a minute ago."

"Good girl," said Mr. Ronkoop and busied himself putting up the camp beds and unstrapping the bedding rolls.

Meanwhile Gilda had gone a couple of hundred yards down the road and was feeling a little despondent. The country looked so dry, there couldn't possible be a creek anywhere for miles. She almost wished she had not started out, as it would be awful to have to go back again without finding water now.

She heard the sound of a car starting off; that must mean her father had finished talking to that brown-faced man. She hurried on. But the car slowed again as it drew level with her.

"Where do you reckon you're off to then?" the man called out.

"Fetching some water," said Gilda, and tried to sound confident about it.

"Fond of walking?"

She shrugged her shoulders. "I don't mind," she said.

"That's good then," he said. "It'd be about seven miles to the next place where you'd be likely to get any water."

"Oh!" said Gilda and stopped. A ridiculous tear somehow or other popped out of one eye and ran down her cheek. She managed to brush it away while pretending to put a strand of hair back.

"You've got three choices, cobber," the man said. "Number one, you can walk; number two, you can do without the water altogether until tomorrow; number three, you can hop in this car and I'll take you to Prentice's place which is the next homestead I was telling you about. But you'll have to take your chance on getting a lift back."

Gilda only hesitated a moment and then said, "Please, I should like to come with you."

The man opened the door for her, took the water carrier and put it over into the back. "Your parents won't be worried?"

"Oh no," said Gilda, wondering what in fact they would say about it.

"Okay, you're the boss," the man said, and the car moved smoothly away.

In a very few minutes it seemed the car slowed down again and stopped by a mailbox on a post at the side of the road. The box was really an old oil drum on its side and painted white. On it was printed in large red letters the name V. PRENTICE.

"Straight up the drive," the man said. "The house is behind the trees there. Real nice place, too. Good luck, cobber."

"Thank you very much for the ride," said Gilda politely.

"Nothing to it," he said. "See you!" and grinned and drove off.

Gilda gripped the handle of the water carrier and faced the long curving drive and the wide-open gates. "All you've got to do now," she said to herself, "is ask." And she began to walk up the drive but keeping to the edge because that didn't look quite so cheeky as marching up the middle.

Halfway along the road humped up to pass over a channel of brown water about twelve feet wide. This, she knew, was an irrigation channel and used to irrigate the farmland, whole fields being flooded when necessary.

She was about to pass on when something

round, like a football floating on the water, attracted her attention and she stopped to stare at it. Then she realized that it was not a ball but someone's head seen from the back and that the someone was swimming in the channel.

The head turned and a pair of brown eyes were looking at her with surprise. Then a boy's voice said anxiously, "Where the blazes did you spring from?"

Gilda began to explain but the boy did not listen. "Don't stand there," he said rather sharply. "Go on, can't you?"

Gilda felt annoyed. "Why shouldn't I stay here if I like?" she said.

"Because I want to get out of the water," the boy said.

"Well, I'm not stopping you."

"Oh yes you are. My word, aren't girls stupid? Don't you realize I haven't got my swimming tights on? I wasn't to know a flaming Sheila was going to come prancing along."

Gilda said, "I'm not allowed to say 'flaming' because it's not ladylike."

The boy groaned. "That's right," he said. "Stand there and natter about nothing while I sink to my death in the mud."

"Don't be silly," Gilda said. "You can

swim." He did seem an odd sort of boy.

The boy sank slowly in the water before her eyes. The water rose over his mouth then over his nose. Just his brown eyes regarded her above the water. They seemed to hold a look of agonized appeal.

"Don't," Gilda cried. "I'm going, really I am."

"Glub-glup. Bubble-bubble-bubble," went the disappearing head. Gilda turned and ran the next twenty yards up the drive and then stopped to listen. At first she heard nothing and wondered if she ought to run back and dive in to save him. Maybe he couldn't swim. Then she heard splashing noises like a large dog coming ashore and she breathed a sigh of relief.

She had gone on a few steps when there was a shout behind her and the boy was standing up on the bank waving. She was relieved to see that he had a pair of blue shorts on.

"Well, wait on, can't you?" he bawled.

"I like that," Gilda said. "First you say go on and then you say wait. Can't you make up your mind?"

The boy only grinned and ran up the road toward her. Gilda thought he was probably younger than she was. About ten, she thought. He was thin but very wiry and brown and had a fuzz of hair bleached almost white on his arms and back. He said his name was Garry.

They walked on up the drive together. A few yards further and it took a sharp turn to the right and the house surrounded by trees came into sight. Gilda stopped to admire it.

"It's beautiful," she said. "The most beautiful house I ever saw."

Garry looked at her with surprise. "Gee!" he said, "it's just a house; nothing to go on about. I've always lived here, and so has my dad. He was born here. We've been here hundreds of years, I reckon."

This was almost more than Gilda could believe. She studied the house with renewed interest. It was a sprawling place, not at all tidy and square like the houses she usually drew. There was a sort of tower, for example, high up above the rest of the house, with an overhanging balcony all round it; there were wings of the house that started out in one direction and then turned suddenly in another, and the piece of land caught in the bend was paved with colored tiles, so that it was a sort of outdoor room, a room without a ceiling.

"My grandfather built the tower," Garry said, "so he could look out over his land. Watch out for fires and so on. Now it's my room."

"Right up there?" said Gilda. "Aren't you afraid it might blow down in the night?"

"It's steady as a rock," Garry boasted. "The beams in it are over a foot thick. Come and see if you like."

Gilda went quite dizzy at the thought of it and followed the boy in without another word.

Real Queer

GILDA could not remember going right inside a house before and she found it not only queer and exciting but a little frightening and creepy as well. To start with, the Prentices had Venetian blinds over each window and this made it oddly dark. Even worse there were parts of the house without windows at all, like long caves or tunnels. There were carpets on the floor so that your feet made no sound, and there were odd smells of clothing and dust, and of things that had happened days or even weeks before. These smells hung in little clouds about the house, instead of being blown right through as they would have been in a tent, and you passed from one little cloud to the next.

Garry took Gilda straight through the house to the center and halted at the foot of a spiral iron staircase.

"This goes up to my room," he said.

Gilda stood at the foot of the staircase and looked upward. The stairs went right round twice and then ended in a sort of platform. They looked safe enough, so she began to go up.

"There are twenty-one stairs," Garry said.

"Why?" asked Gilda.

"I don't know, there just are. I was telling you for interest."

"If I'd wanted to know I could have counted them."

"Sorry," Garry said.

Gilda decided she would count them and stopped to look back and see how many she had already climbed. Then she went on.

"Gee, girls!" Garry muttered.

"Well," said Gilda at the top, "there were only twenty, so there!"

"Not if you count the top one."

"The top one isn't a stair, it's the floor."

"It's a stair until you get to the top."

"It's just the floor."

"You have to lift your foot to get to it."

Gilda considered for a moment and then said, "Then you ought to count the floor at the bottom as well, and that would make twenty-two, so you're still wrong."

"You do count the bottom if you're going downstairs, but then you don't count the top one."

"Why?"

"Because," said Garry, absolutely exasperated, "That's the way you have to count stairs."

"Nonsense!" said Gilda. "That's just the way *you* count them. It doesn't mean *I* have to."

"Do you always argue about everything?"

"I wasn't arguing," said Gilda indignantly. "You were arguing. I was just showing you how you were wrong."

Garry sighed. "Well, this is my room," he said. It was not a big room but it was very light and full of sunshine, and having four large windows or glass doors seemed to let the trees right into the room. It was like living in the treetops, yet with all the protection and comfort of a house.

"This is lovely," said Gilda.

"Get's pretty hot," Garry said. Because it was his room he felt he could not say how much he liked it — and he was very fond of it — but must quickly point out the disadvantages, even exaggerate them a little.

"I shouldn't mind that," Gilda said. "If ever I do live in a proper house I'm going to have a room just like this."

Garry looked puzzled. "Don't you live in a proper house then?" he asked.

"No, I never have. Well, not since I was

very little and I can't remember that properly."

Garry stared at her and then grinned broadly. "Go on," he said, "you're kidding, aren't you?"

"No, it's the truth. We live in a tent and travel round the different places for Dad to get to work. It's all right really."

"All right!" exclaimed Garry. "I reckon it'd be bonza. Like always being on holiday. I only stay all the time in this stuffy old house and see the same things all the time. Gee, I wish I was you."

This was quite a new idea to Gilda. "I suppose it is quite fun in a way," she said, "all the same . . . oh, I don't know."

"It's because you're a girl, I expect," Garry said wisely. "Girls are pretty cranky about some things . . ."

"They are not," said Gilda fiercely.

"Oh, you know what I mean. A bloke would be pretty pleased to just wander around, going on when he got tired of a place, or staying if he liked it. But girls always want floors to polish and stoves and washing machines and all that junk."

Gilda was so cross she didn't know what to say first. And while she was spluttering like a tomato in a frying pan there was a sudden crash from downstairs.

"Who left this flaming can in the passage?" a man's voice shouted angrily.

"That's Dad," said Garry.

"What is it, dear? Have you fallen over something?" said a woman's voice from farther away.

"And that's Mum," said Garry.

"And that was probably my water carrier he fell over," said Gilda. "I left it somewhere at the bottom of the stairs."

"Fell over!" shouted the man. "Didn't you hear me? Break both my legs and crack my head open and you say, 'Have you fallen over something?' Are you deaf or something?"

"I think I'd better go down," said Gilda.

"Why?"

"Well, it was my fault. And if he has broken his legs . . ."

"Not him," said Garry. "He's just making a fuss about nothing, the way grownups always do. He's really cross with himself for not seeing your can, and instead of blaming himself for being so clumsy, he has to shout at everybody else. He'll get over it."

Gilda looked at Garry with amazement. She had never heard anyone speak about parents in this way before. Of course he was probably right; she often thought the same sort of thing, but never spoke her thoughts aloud. Garry on the other hand did not seem at all perturbed but sat on the side of his bed swinging his legs and looking out of the window.

"Take a walk round the balcony," he suggested. "It's nice out there. We'll go down again in a while. Give Dad a chance to cool off."

So Gilda took his advice and went out on the balcony and admired the rich green of the trees all round the house and the lawns and orchards which she now discovered lay behind. When she went back into the room Garry got up off his bed. "Okay," he said. "I reckon we could go down now."

Gilda was rather nervous of doing this; it seemed like going into a lion's cage a few minutes after the lion had finished growling. However, she had to go down sooner or later, so it would be silly to make a fuss about it.

And Mr. Prentice turned out to be short and tubby and not at all like the sound of his voice. They came on him, when Gilda had filled her water carrier, sitting outside on the veranda, stuffing himself with ripe apricots. He was sitting forward on a low cane chair looking hot and pink in undershirt and khaki shorts, large muddy boots but no socks. He had a battered felt hat pushed to the back of his head. The whole of his attention was being given to a large bowl of apricots.

"Dad, this is Gilda," Garry said.

Mr. Prentice made some sort of noise that must have been intended as a greeting.

"She lives in a tent," Barry said, "and she came to ask for some water."

Gilda was afraid of the mention of water would remind Mr. Prentice of his fall, but he merely said, "Where are you camping then?" and popped another apricot into his mouth.

"About seven miles back," said Gilda. "The car broke down so we had to stop."

"Um," said Mr. Prentice. "That far, eh? Well, you can't walk that; I'd better drive you down."

He stood up and hitched at his shorts, then on second thoughts picked up the bowl of apricots and led the way down the veranda steps carrying it with him. As he was going, Mrs. Prentice's voice from somewhere inside the house called out, "Ted, have you seen anything of those apricots I put in the blue bowl? I thought I'd make jam of them."

Mr. Prentice looked at the bowl he was carrying and saw it was blue. Then he said to Garry, "Tell your mother I've just gone down the road," and hurried over toward the large gleaming car parked in the shade of a golden willow tree. Gilda hurried after him.

"Hold those," he said, thrusting the apricots on her lap as soon as she sat down, and he started the car with a jerk that spat gravel right up on the veranda.

As they drove along the road Mr. Prentice kept reaching his hand over and dipping for another apricot, and not until the bowl was nearly empty did he glance at Gilda and say, "You're a rum kid. Don't you like apricots then?"

"Yes," said Gilda. "I like them very much."

"Why aren't you eating 'em then?"

She thought it might sound rude to say, "Because you didn't offer me one," so she just murmured, "Thank you," and took one. Only just in time, she thought, as his hand came dipping across again. And in fact by the time she had eaten two the bowl was empty.

Mr. Prentice sighed and licked his fingers. "I don't know," he said. "There's something *about* apricots . . . is that your camp?"

It was. As he swung his car in a wide circle in the road he said, "Reckon you could have chosen a better place than that."

"We didn't choose it," said Gilda. "The car broke down."

"Oh yes, you told me."

When she got out he drove off before she had time to thank him properly, merely pushing his hat back farther on his head, so that it looked more like a halo than a hat.

Mrs. Ronkoop showed how worried she had been by being very angry with Gilda for at least half an hour.

"I don't know how many times I've told you not to take rides in strangers' cars," she said.

"Well, I did get some water," said Gilda. "And I'm all right, aren't I?"

"But that's not the point. It is disobedience. To do something when you know — and another time you might not be all right."

And so she went on for quite a while. Gilda thought to herself that it was all very unfair, and no one had thanked her for all the trouble she had been to. Of course it just showed how fond her mother was of her. But there must be better ways of showing it. Then thinking it was time they talked about something else, she said cheerfully, "I've been right inside a house. It was real queer. But nice too. And this boy had his room up in a tower."

"You and your houses," said her mother. "I don't believe you've been listening to a word I've been telling you. Which boy?"

"Garry," said Gilda.

"Oh, so now we have Garry in a tower. What are you telling me about?"

Gilda thought to herself that this wasn't a very good subject either, so she said, "What's for tea?"

"It's your favorite," said Mrs. Ronkoop, but still in a grumpy voice. "Ham omelette and chips. Though you don't deserve it, going off like that without a single word . . ."

Ronnie and Robyn

M R. RONKOOP said it wasn't going to rain
and he was right. They slept out in the open
with the clear black sky overhead and the
bright sharp stars behind the lattice of gum
leaves. Living in the open had its compen-
sations; in the darkness of a house there
was nothing to do but close your eyes and go
to sleep, but in the open you could lie, gradually getting drowsier, watching the stars
and listening to the quiet night noises. The
tiny scratching of the possums' feet in the
treebark made the darkness fidgety with
life. The boobook owls calling and answer-
ing could be heard more than a mile away.

The next morning, because there were no
tents to take down and fold, they were
packed up long before the man from the
garage arrived with his breakdown truck
to tow them away.

The garage was in a small township ten
miles up the road. There was a tall yellow

stone water tower, a hotel much in need of some paint, a tiny disused stone church with all the windows broken, three shops, one of which was also the post office, three private houses and the garage.

Mrs. Ronkoop walked down the street on one side and back on the other. When she got to the garage again Mr. Ronkoop was shouting at the garage man and waving his hands about in a very excited way. Mrs. Ronkoop joined in after a while, but Gilda went quickly back down the street and stared for at least ten minutes into a window before realizing that it was not a shop but one of the ordinary houses. The trouble was she always got so embarrassed when her parents acted like foreigners that she didn't know what she was doing.

This was odd because Gilda was proud of being Dutch and of knowing a bit more about the world than most of the children she met at school.

A little later she looked back toward the garage and saw that her parents had walked out into the road and were having a very serious discussion. It was obviously so serious that it could only be about money. She was going down to join them and find out, when Mr. Ronkoop suddenly flung out his hands and stamped back to the garage.

Gilda knew that gesture; it meant that Mr. Ronkoop had been forced to do something very much against his will but from which there was no escape. So she went back to her mother and asked her what had gone wrong.

Mrs. Ronkoop shrugged her shoulders and said, "*Ja, ja,* such crazy," which wasn't much help.

A few minutes later Gilda knew what had happened for Mr. Ronkoop came round from the back of the garage driving a different car altogether, connected their trailer up to it, and came along the road toward them. It was obvious he had traded their old car for this one.

They got in and drove away and for the next half an hour there was a glum silence. Gilda couldn't understand it. The new car seemed better in every way than the old. It didn't make such a dreadful rattling noise and it didn't smell of burning oil as the old one had. The seats were much more comfortable and the windows all went up and down properly instead of getting stuck halfway and letting the rain in. As far as she could see it was an all-round improvement.

At last she could stand the silence no longer, so she said to her father, "I think I'm glad the old car broke down. This one is much better."

Mr. Ronkoop snorted through his nose like a horse that has been frightened by a piece of newspaper flapping in the wind. "So it should be," he said. "Two hundred and forty dollars better."

"Such crazy," agreed Mrs. Ronkoop. "But what others could you do?"

"We have to have a car," said Mr. Ronkoop.

"*Ja, ja,*" said Mrs. Ronkoop, nodding her head. Then she folded her arms very tight across her middle and looked grimly at the road ahead. Silence descended on the family once again as they drove onward.

Gilda found that she did not want to speak either; she had suddenly realized that her father had spent all that money on a car, and that it was some of the very eight hundred he had been saving toward buying a house one day.

Another hour's driving brought them to the first of the vineyards and Gilda began to think of Ronnie and Robyn Brunt, her friends, whom she had not seen for months.

Mr. Ronkoop did not drive into Mildura but went straight to the vineyards owned by two brothers named Staros and Evados Minopolous, two New Australians from

Greece. This was where the Ronkoops and the Brunts worked every year, and it was always understood that they should meet there. There was even a special corner of one of the vineyards, a flat triangle of green grass shaded by a row of poplar trees, where they always camped.

As they turned off the road and made their way slowly up the bumpy track between the vines Gilda began to get excited. She sat as high as she could and turned her head quickly from side to side, so as not to miss any of the familiar sights.

There was the old horse called Charlie that was sometimes used to bring in the grapes when the ground was too wet and gluey for the tractors, and there were the two tame white cockatoos called Castor and Pollux strutting up and down in the dust, raising and lowering their yellow crests and squabbling as usual, and there was . . . Gilda sighed contentedly; everything was in the right place and as it should be. It was almost like coming home.

They bumped farther and farther through the vines. The tops of the poplar trees could be seen now; one more turning and they would be able to see if the Brunts had arrived yet.

As the car turned left round the corner

there was an ear-splitting, soul-shattering yell which seemed to come from right under the front wheels of the car. Mr. Ronkoop jammed on the brakes. Mrs. Ronkoop who was nearest the window cried, "It's the children! Gilda, look!"

A boy and a girl, both as brown as tree trunks, were squatting on the edge of a drainage channel and grinning up at the car.

"Gilda!" the boy shouted. "Come and catch crayfish! They're bigger than ever this year!"

Gilda climbed over her mother and scrambled down the bank. The Brunt children had already returned to their fishing and did not look up again as she squattted beside them.

"I haven't any cotton or bait," she said.

Ronnie was hauling cautiously on one of his lines. He held it steady with his left hand, the piece of steak just beneath the surface, and approached the crayfish with his right hand under the water. Then he snatched quickly, catching the creature with forefinger and thumb just behind the joints of the sharp nippers. "Seventeen," he said with satisfaction, dropping it into the rusty can by his side. "There's some cotton in my pocket and some bait in the tin."

He threw the bait well out, put a bare foot

on the cotton and began to haul in the next line. Gilda inserted two fingers into his pocket and found the cotton.

About ten minutes and three crayfish later Robyn said, "School started last Tuesday; you missed four days."

"What's it like this year?" asked Gilda.

"We haven't been yet," said Ronnie. "Mum said we needn't start till you arrived. What did you have to come in such a hurry for? We were hoping you'd be at least a week yet."

Gilda stared very fixedly at her line which began to go fuzzy and blurred. Robyn gave her a quick glance and then scowled at her brother, but he noticed nothing. "Pull your line in, you nong," he said. "You've got a crayfish there eating all your bait!"

Gilda dropped the line altogether and climbed the bank clumsily. As she hurried away to where she could see her father with the tent already half up she heard Robyn saying:

"Fancy saying a thing like that! I think you're hateful."

"Like what?" came Ronnie's surprised voice.

A few seconds later Gilda heard Robyn's feet pattering along behind her and then a warm wet hand grabbed hers and hung on.

Gilda squeezed it slightly and thought, Robyn's nice. I don't know why I wanted to get to Mildura so quickly. And that boy Garry was much nicer than Ronnie. I hate this place. It's always so hot and there are always so many insects. I wish we never had to come here.

Mrs. Brunt had already made a pot of tea and poured some for Gilda when she came up. "Two spoonfuls of sugar," she said. "I remember. But isn't it *nice* being all together again. I don't know *how* many times Ronnie and Robyn have asked me when do I think you'll come."

There was an explosive Dutch noise from the inside of the Ronkoop's tent.

"What did your father say?" asked Mrs. Brunt.

"He was really swearing," said Gilda.

"Then it's just as well I don't understand Dutch, isn't it?" said Mrs. Brunt. "Oh dear, do you think he's hurt himself?"

"He is always hurting himself," said Mrs. Ronkoop. "He is that sort of man."

Mr. Brunt, a lean stringy man with an eternally sad face, ducked out of his own tent and called, "Wait on, old cobber! Just on my way."

He fought his way into the swaying green mass that ought to have been square and upright by now. Immediately it collapsed completely and two queer-shaped humps, one tall and thin, the other short and fat, heaved about under the canvas. Mr. Brunt emerged first rubbing his head.

"Go in there and help my old mate," he exclaimed, "and what does he do? Clobbers me over the head with the flaming tent pole."

Mr. Ronkoop stood up and pulled the canvas off his shoulders like the beggar in the fairy story throwing off his rags and revealing himself to be a real prince.

"Oh my good friends," he cried. "How unlucky a man I am!"

"You unlucky?" said Mr. Brunt. "I thought I was the one that got clobbered."

Mrs. Ronkoop was clucking like a hen with chicks, taking it all very seriously, but Mrs. Brunt had tears streaming from her eyes and was laughing as if she was watching a comedy turn.

"You two!" she exclaimed. "You ought to be on TV. If only you could see yourselves."

By and by the two men attacked the tent again and got it up properly, and while the two women unpacked the Ronkoops' trailer, they went up to the house to see the Minopolus brothers to find out when the picking was likely to start.

Ronnie came up from the dam with his can of crayfish. He did not even look at the girls but said to his mother:

"Have you finished with the primus, Mum?"

"Why?"

"I just thought I'd cook these crayfish. I got thirty or forty; not sure exactly how many."

"That will be nice with our tea," Mrs. Brunt said.

Ronnie put the can on the stove and stood staring down at it.

Robyn said, "Do you have to stand there gloating over them while the poor things die?"

"You're cranky," he said. "You catch them and you eat them, but you can't stand anyone killing them. I keep telling you this is the kindest way. When the water gets warm all the air is driven out and they drown. Only takes a few seconds."

"I know," said Robyn. "But you don't have to *watch* them drowning."

"What difference does it make if I watch them?"

"It's cruel."

"Aw gee! Aren't girls stupid!"

Gilda said, "I met a boy yesterday who kept saying that. He showed me over his house and he's got a room up in a tower. It was just about the best sort of room you could have."

"What was he like?" asked Robyn.

"He was quite good-looking really," said Gilda. "He was called Garry and he had fair hair and brown eyes and he's a very good swimmer . . ."

Robyn suddenly giggled, and when Gilda looked at her to see why, Robyn pointed at her brother who had walked away from the stove and had picked up the water carrier.

"I'll just go and fill this, Mum," he said, and marched off with it.

"Whatever's the matter with him?" said Mrs. Brunt. "He hates getting water usually. I have to tell him half a dozen times before he'll go."

Robyn giggled again and nudged Gilda. "Tell me some more about this boy you met," she said.

"Oh," said Gilda, "there isn't any more to tell. He was quite ordinary, really." And she watched Ronnie striding out along the track, swinging the water carrier as he went.

Charlie to the Rescue

THE MINOPOPOLUS BROTHERS said they were starting on Monday; Mrs. Ronkoop and Mrs. Brunt decided that the children ought to start school on Monday also, and then they went over to the dried-fruit factory and arranged to start work themselves on the same day packing raisins.

That was how life was at Mildura each year; it had a regular pattern. For about six weeks everybody went about things in a steady and rhythmical way. They all got up in the mornings at six, had breakfast, and went to work at half past seven. The children did a few jobs about the camp until eight and then took their time getting to school. Often they did the previous night's homework in the morning, because it was quiet and cool then and better for concentration.

At half past six in the evening they had a

huge meal — the main meal of the day, a sort of dinner and tea combined. Then they played cards or talked for an hour or so and went to bed fairly early.

Gilda liked life to be this way. She liked to be among people she knew. It was more the way ordinary people lived. In fact, apart from the oddity of having canvas walls to their house, they really were ordinary people.

The only thing she did not enjoy was being in the same class at school. "I'm sorry," the teacher said, "but I can't put you up into grade five, Gilda. You couldn't do the work yet."

Gilda tried not to show her disappointment, but a few tears would creep out.

"I know it's not your fault," the teacher said. "You're a good pupil. I remember your work from last year. But it's all this moving about. You lose a lot of time, you see. And then schools are different and it takes you more time to settle down. And then just when you are used to us and might make some progress, off you go again."

"I know," said Gilda. "Oh, well . . ."

Yes, that was the bad part, doing the same school work over and over again. And the teacher was quite right; Gilda still could not do long division yet, and she read very slowly for her age, and made silly mistakes over simple words. And her spelling! Her compositions sometimes looked as if they were written in a foreign language.

So back Gilda had to go into grade four where most of the children were at least two years younger than she was. The only consolation she had was that the teacher did not bother her much. As she would be gone again in a few weeks she was left to work mostly on her own.

The other children looked on her as a bit of an oddity. She was used to that, for it was the same in every school she went to. Ronnie and Robyn had the same trouble, of course, and it was a comfort to them all to have each other. In the midday recess they always met and managed to forget about school, and after half past three everything was all right again.

In any case all this became quite unimportant when the trouble started, which was when the Ronkoops and the Brunts had been working for less than a fortnight.

The Minopolous' vineyard was only a small one of about twenty acres, and the Minopolous brothers, who both had large families, did not employ more than half a dozen pickers. Every year on one or other of the large vineyards there was some sort of trouble about the amount of money the pickers were to be paid for their work. Often the pickers went on strike for more money, and quite often there was a bit of fighting here and there before things were arranged to everybody's satisfaction.

This did not usually make any difference to the Minopolous pickers, who made their own arrangements with the brothers. But this year, however, it was a different story.

Toward the end of the second week, around half past seven in the evening, when the two families had just finished their tea and were squabbling in a friendly fashion about whose turn it was to do the dishes, three men suddenly appeared at the camp and stood in a row in front of the tents.

Mr. Brunt looked up. "How're you doing?" he said in a friendly manner.

One of the men, a short muscular man dressed in bleached blue jeans and a grubby undershirt, glanced at his two companions and then said:

"How much are you getting paid?"

"I don't know what business it is of yours," said Brunt, still pleasantly.

"We happen to be making it our business," said the man in blue jeans.

"That's right," said the man on his right, and then coughed as if the effort had hurt his throat.

"We don't look for trouble," said Mr. Ronkoop.

"That's right, mate," said the man in blue jeans. "I just asked a civil question."

"Three dollars the hundred is what we have agreed," said Mr. Ronkoop. The bunches of grapes were usually picked into small metal trays ready for the driers which turned them into raisins. The two men generally packed about five hundred of these trays a day.

"Three dollars?" said the man. "I thought as much. It's not enough."

"It's what we fixed," said Mr. Brunt, "A bargain is a bargain. And if we're satisfied, what's it got to do with you?"

"Us pickers have to stick together," said the man. "We've gone on strike for another fifty cents a hundred. You'd better do the same."

Brunt said, "That'll be the day — when I take orders from you, matie."

"*Na, na,*" said Mr. Ronkoop. "We don't want any sort of trouble about these things."

"Well, I've told you," said the man. "Be healthier for you to take notice."

"That's right," said the other man and coughed again. Then they all three turned about and marched off.

There was an argument then among the four grownups which Gilda did not properly understand. In the end both men came to the conclusion that it was nothing to do with the other pickers what they did, and that they would go to work the next morning as usual.

The following day after school the three children went up to the vineyard instead of having their usual swim in the pool. They found their fathers still picking. Nothing had been seen of the pickers on strike and no more had been said about stopping work.

"It was just a bit of stupid bluff," said Mr. Brunt. "Here, good thing you kids turned up. Would you like to earn fifty cents each?"

"How?" said Ronnie suspiciously.

"Go and harness up old Charlie to the float and bring him down here. The tractor's not back from the driers yet, and we want this lot carried in before we finish, or it won't be tallied for today."

The children liked driving Charlie and would have done it without being paid. They ran up to the farm to collect the harness and carried it down to the paddock where Charlie was standing doing nothing but gazing soulfully into the distance over the gate.

Getting the harness on was not easy. The horse was too tall for any of them to reach properly, and it was only when Gilda held Charlie's head and urged him close up to the gate that Ronnie was able to stand on the top bar and lean over to fix the straps on the collar.

The harness was very old and worn, mended with bits of wire and strings. Parts of it seemed quite unnecessary until the children found out exactly how it was supposed to go. But Charlie was very patient and stood still while they clambered all over him and ducked underneath him trying different ways. Every now and again he swung his head round and took a look at the mess they were making of it.

After about twenty minutes of struggling they had everything fixed and backed him between the shafts of the float and hung the chains on the hooks of his collar.

"Well, it may not be quite right," Ronnie said, "but if he goes forward the cart is bound to follow. And that's what counts."

Then they all climbed on the float and Ronnie shook the rope that acted as the reins and Charlie leaned forward and started to amble along as soon as he was sure the float was following. Ronnie stood up, keeping his balance, although the float pitched from side to side in the ruts. Gilda half got to her feet thinking to copy him but thought how silly she would look if she fell off and sat down again.

Robyn gave her a quick smile and said, "I think it's much more fun sitting down, anyway."

They reached the end of the row where their fathers were picking, loaded up the float with trays of grapes and took them up to the shed where fruit was stored overnight. When they had unloaded they began the return journey.

As soon as Charlie turned out of the yard Ronnie exclaimed, "There's those men again. Only there's about a dozen of them this time. I bet it means trouble."

"Where?" Gilda clutched Ronnie's arm and stood up on the float, helping Robyn up with her other hand.

"They've got bottles in their hands," Robyn said. "I expect they've just come along for a friendly drink."

Somehow Gilda didn't think the men looked at all friendly. They had entered the field from the top end, about six rows from where Mr. Ronkoop and Mr. Brunt were working, and split up into two groups, one down each side. Old Charlie ambled steadily on without any help from Ronnie, making his way back again.

By the time the float was at the bottom of the field the men had reached the ends of the row the two friends were picking. They turned and began to march inward. Mr. Ronkoop saw them first and stopped picking. He said something to his friend. They both moved away from the vines and stood in the open, back to back. Mr. Brunt suddenly bent down, picked up a couple of empty grape trays and gave one to Mr. Ronkoop as a weapon.

"There's going to be a fight!" said Gilda. "And it's not fair; all those against just two. Can't we do something?"

Ronnie had been standing as if hypnotized all this while. Gilda's voice seemed to wake him up. He grabbed the reins tight in both hands and shook them. "Come on, Charlie boy!" he cried.

Charlie jerked his head up as if amazed, but nevertheless he increased his pace to a sort of shuffle. When Ronnie shook the reins again Charlie began to canter.

The float leapt wildly over the rough track

and the children had to hang on as best they could. In a few seconds they were at the end of the row and had turned into it.

The first thing the children saw was their fathers facing a ring of men. It was obvious now that the bottles had not been brought out of friendship but as weapons. One of the men actually had his raised in the air like a club.

Ronnie turned the ends of the reins over and beat Charlie across the rump. "Go on!" he shouted.

Charlie fairly leapt forward between the vines, the float thundering behind, straight for the circle of men.

Paid Off

GILDA never really saw what happened after that. Lying almost flat on the leaping, pitching float, she had vivid flashes of Charlie's head plunging up and down and his coarse, tangled mane flapping in a lump on his neck, then at one moment when she was thrown sideways she had a glimpse of startled faces as the men heard the clatter of the float and the thunder of Charlie's huge hoofs. She saw some of them pushing and ducking under the vines to get out of the way. She heard shouts.

Then there was a crash and a jar as the corner of the float struck a stack of trays full of grapes, and for a moment the air seemed full of flying bunches. Then they were through.

Gilda looked back expecting to see half a dozen men crushed in the dirt, but they all seemed to have leaped to safety. They shouted after the children and two of them threw empty beer bottles, one of which hit the float and bounced off without breaking.

A few more seconds and Charlie reached the end of the row, turned and slowed down to a lumbering trot. Ronkoop and Brunt appeared at the side and leaped for the float as it passed and managed to scramble on. They were both out of breath, but neither of them was hurt.

"You arrived in the nick of time, I think," Mr. Ronkoop said.

"Good for you, kids," said Mr. Brunt. "They would have clobbered the daylights out of us."

They drove the float back to camp and kept Charlie down there for a while. The two men went quickly to their tents and reappeared with their sporting guns just in case the strikers had the idea of following them and continuing the argument.

Everything was quiet after that, however, and when Mrs. Ronkoop and Mrs. Brunt came back from the packing sheds they said there was no one in the vineyards except one of the Minopolous brothers, who seemed very worried and wanted to talk to one or the other of the two men.

Mr. Brunt went up, taking Charlie and the float with him. When he came back half an hour later he had a very glum expression. He handed Mr. Ronkoop an envelope containing a roll of notes and some loose silver.

"What's this?" exclaimed Mr. Ronkoop.

"Paid off!" said Brunt briefly. "Finished."

"There is three or four weeks' work left yet!"

"Too right, cobber. But not for us. Old Minopolous says he can't afford to pay three fifty a hundred, and on account of the troubles in the other vineyards he's not taking the chance of paying less, so he's going to finish the picking with his family. Seems there's another brother with three grown kids, and they'll come up from Melbourne and give him a hand."

"But we are finished?"

"Afraid so. Of course there's nothing to stop us from going down to one or another of the bigger vineyards and getting jobs at the new rates."

"There was a job going in the drying sheds this morning," said Mrs. Brunt.

They argued it out over the evening meal and in the end the Brunts decided to stay if Mr. Brunt could get the job at the drying sheds, and the Ronkoops made up their minds to move on. The children were not asked for their opinion.

Gilda cried silently in her bed for nearly an hour before she fell asleep. The period at Mildura was the one part of the year she really looked forward to, and here it was finished already after only a fortnight. During the night she was so restless that she woke her mother up.

"What is it? What's the matter?" said Mrs. Ronkoop, thinking that Gilda was ill.

Gilda did not wake but turned restlessly and muttered, "It's not fair. It's not fair!"

Mrs. Ronkoop grunted and went back to bed.

The next day was Saturday. Gilda had hoped that her parents would stay in Mildura for the weekend, and perhaps they could all have gone for a trip on the old river paddle boat, the *Coonawara,* as they usually did some time while at Mildura. But Mr. Ronkoop was worried about money. He wanted to move straight away so as to find work by Monday.

So the tent was down and the trailer packed before midday.

"See you sometime," said Mr. Brunt.

"If you come on something really good, let us know," said Mrs. Brunt. "Maybe we could join up again later this year." She glanced quickly at the children as if to say it would be nicer for them to be together. Ronnie turned away and started fossicking around by the tent.

"Where's my bait?" he said angrily. "I'm going crayfishing."

"Aren't you going to say good-bye?" said his mother.

"I've already said good-bye," he growled. "I can't stand all this mush."

Then he found his bait and reel of black cotton and made off toward his favorite bend in the drainage channel.

"He's very sorry really," said Mrs. Brunt to Gilda. "You know what boys are."

Mr. Ronkoop started the car. "Well," he said.

Everybody babbled at once and waved. Then the Ronkoops drove off and in a few seconds turned at the corner of the track and the camp disappeared from sight. Ronnie looked up as the car passed him and gave a sort of a grin.

"I've caught two already," he shouted and held a large black crayfish up for Gilda's inspection. He wasn't holding it carefully enough and it fastened a nipper on his finger. He gave a howl and dropped the creature back in the tin, and the last sight Gilda had of him was of a wild figure capering about on the mud and sucking a damaged finger. Gilda laughed and then sank back on the seat and stared dully in front.

"That Ronnie!" said Mrs. Ronkoop. "Such crazy!"

They drove through the brassy heat. The long straight road shimmered with pools of distant water which vanished as they approached. The sheep in the flat dry paddocks lay crowded close against the trunks of large old gum trees. Only the cicadas and the Ronkoops' car seemed to have energy enough for noise and movement. Everything else was still in the heat.

The car moved gradually off the bitumen on to the dust at the side and then was jerked back. It did this three times and then Mr. Ronkoop said, "This won't do; I'm nodding asleep. I think we'd better stop for a while."

He drew the car off the road just near a notice that said FIREPLACE and pointed to a concrete construction on the cleared patch.

"Just a little sleep, then a cup of tea and we go on again," he said, and getting out of the car he found a comfortable place on a sloping bank and settled down. He put his hat right over his face to keep the flies off and was fast asleep in a few minutes.

"In a little while maybe," said Mrs. Ronkoop, "you make a nice fire in the fireplace and your father will have a drink of tea when he wakes, yes?"

Gilda looked around for some wood and found three small dead branches under the tree. As it did not need much to boil a billy she did not bother to look farther. Instead she sat down and watched a pair of brightly colored parakeets searching very thoroughly up and down the bark of a dead limb. Just like a couple of kids, she thought, that had dropped a nickel and couldn't buy any lollipops until they had found it. Now and then one of them tore a strip of the loose brittle bark off the tree and let it drop with a crackling sound to the ground.

By and by Gilda's mother lit a fire and when the water in the billy was boiling she woke Mr. Ronkoop. While they were all sipping the hot tea a large mob of sheep, five hundred or more, came into sight in the distance and approached slowly, grazing on the wide verges as they came. Two horsemen moved slowly behind them; two dogs kept the mob clear of the actual roadway, so that the occasional car or truck had no difficulty in passing.

Mrs. Ronkoop put the billy on again.

"I don't want any more," said Mr. Ron-koop. "I'm all right now."

Mrs. Ronkoop pointed to the two men on horseback. "I reckon those two will be having a fine thirst."

The sheep passed slowly, a few pausing to stare at them, and one old ewe to stamp her front feet at them, but the rest going to either side as they would a rock or a fallen tree.

Mrs. Ronkoop called at the riders, "Can you stop for a cup of tea?"

"Too right we can," said one. He gave instructions to one of the tousled brown sheep dogs to "Keep 'em going, Jess!" and then both men rode over.

"Why," one exclaimed as he dismounted, "if it isn't the little lady that likes apricots!"

Gilda thought this was most unfair, but she smiled and said, "Hullo, Mr. Prentice." And when she saw her parents looking mystified she explained how they had met the day the old car broke down.

Mr. Prentice and his drover squatted on their heels and drank their tea, and because there did not seem to be much to talk about, Gilda started to tell him of their reason for leaving Mildura. Mr. Prentice was very sympathetic and turning to Mr. Ronkoop said:

"You'll be looking for a job, then?"

"Yes," said Mr. Ronkoop. "As soon as possible."

"Well now," said Mr. Prentice. "I don't know if this would interest you . . ." He went on to explain how he had a half share in a timber mill in the Moogara Forest, and how the manager of the mill had just written asking Mr. Prentice to try and get him a couple of workers.

"It's a bit on the lonely side out there," he added. "Not everybody likes it. But if you'd care to go and look it over . . . well, if you didn't take the job no one would blame you."

Mr. Ronkoop asked a few questions and then said he would certainly go and see. Gilda didn't care for the sound of it at all, having gathered it was in a sort of swamp, miles and miles from anywhere.

As Mr. Prentice was going, and had in fact already mounted his horse, he stopped again. "I forgot one thing," he said. "There's a house there you might be interested in . . ."

"A house?" cried Gilda, getting excited.

"Oh now, don't get the wrong idea. It's pretty rough. Never was more than a two-room shack and only slab-built. I mean it's not a place you would want to live in without a bit of repairing. But if you're interested you can have it for ten dollars a year."

"We pay more than that a week on camp-sites," said Mr. Ronkoop.

"Well, that'd be up to you. The manager will tell you where to find it. Now I'll have to look out for another bloke . . . I suppose you don't know anybody?"

"The Brunts," said Gilda. "They'd come. I'm sure they would."

Mr. Ronkoop looked doubtful. "I think we'd better look at it first," he said. "If it's suitable we could write to them."

"Oh yes," said Gilda. "I'm sure it will be absolutely perfect."

Mr. Prentice laughed. "You, young lady, are in for some very rude shocks, I'm afraid. Moogara Forest is no fairyland, I can assure you."

The House in the Forest

THE MOOGARA FOREST was too far for them to reach that day. When they met Mr. Prentice they had come about eighty miles from Mildura, and Moogara was another hundred and fifty miles farther on.

"It'll work out just about right," said Mr. Ronkoop. "We'll get there tomorrow afternoon and have a look around. That'll be Sunday. If we like the look of it I could start work on Monday."

So they drove for another three hours before camping down for the night by a river, and then went on the next morning, so as to reach the edge of the forest by midday.

All this time they had been traveling on the southern side of the great Murray River, which winds and twists and turns its way along the border between Victoria and New South Wales. The forest lay on the northern bank and filled up all the space of a huge bend in this mighty river. There was no bridge across to it but a ferry pulled by a cable.

The Ronkoops came to the ferry in the sultry heat of midday. The ferry itself, which looked like a piece of a wooden bridge floating on the water, lay over against the far shore. Apart from the quiet murmuring of the river and the very distant clucking of a hen, there was no sound. The air was so still that even the leaves hung limp and motionless. When Mr. Ronkoop switched off the engine it was as if the silence, like great balls of cotton wool, had rolled up from either side and buried them all. They got out of the car whispering to each other and went down to the river bank. There were no houses anywhere; no people in sight.

At the side of the road there was an old ship's bell on a post and above it a sign on which was printed "Ring for Ferry." There was nothing to ring with, so Mr. Ronkoop picked up a piece of rock and banged it on the side of the bell, which gave out an irritated, cracked sound, more like the yapping of a small bad-tempered dog than a proper bell note. A couple of green parrots flew up out of the grass and dashed off protesting, but otherwise nothing happened. Mr. Ronkoop rang the bell again, still without any result.

Gilda went down to the edge of the water and stared at the ferry. On it was a small cabin, no doubt the engine room.

"Perhaps the ferryman is asleep in there," she said. "I could swim over and see."

Mrs. Ronkoop did not like this idea at all, but Mr. Ronkoop said they didn't want to sit there for the rest of the afternoon, and the only other way over the river meant a drive of nearly fifty miles, so why not let the girl try it.

Mrs. Ronkoop muttered and mumbled to herself for a while, and in the end said well, if Gilda got drowned it would be Mr. Ronkoop's fault. So Gilda found her bathing suit in the trailer and changed into it, rather pleased she had thought of the idea, as it would be nice to have a swim and be doing something useful at the same time.

As she was going down to the river again her mother said:

"Wait! What is that noise?"

Squeak, squeak, squeak — pop.

"Like pulling a cork out of a bottle," said Gilda.

Three more corks were popped in quick succession, apparently behind a small bush near the side of the road. Gilda crept over to have a look.

The sudden sound of fiendish, hooting laughter came from the same direction. This ought to have made Gilda jump, but it didn't because she had already caught sight of a dark brown leg and a pink foot. She walked right round the bush, and in the shade on the other side lay a young aboriginal boy, his hands behind his head, his face all teeth in an immense grin.

"Have you been lying there all the time?" demanded Gilda. "Did you hear us ringing the bell?"

The boy put both hands over his mouth and drew his knees right up to his chest in silent laughter. Then he straightened out and began to make a noise like a rubber duck with a squeaker in it when it's pressed too hard. In fact the same noise the big red and gray cockatoos make.

Gilda did not feel like being entertained just then. "We want to cross on the ferry," she said. "Do you know where the ferryman is?"

The boy nodded two or three times and then began to gurgle like a magpie.

"Oh, do stop showing off," said Gilda. "Why didn't the ferryman come when we rang the bell?"

The boy looked solemn. "He's a real lazy bloke," he said. "I don't reckon he'll keep that job long." Then he started drawing corks again.

Gilda walked away in disgust. "He's no use," she said to her parents. "I expect the ferryman is asleep on the ferry. I'll swim across and see."

She waded into the river, which was warm, and swam across. It was quite a long way and the current was stronger than it looked. She had to point herself upstream and swim at an angle, and this in the end brought her to the end of the ferry.

There was no ferryman in the cabin after all; only a small very rusty engine and a wheel on which the cable was wound. Gilda went on to the bank and had a good look under the bushes and in every piece of shade big enough for a man to lie in, but still no ferryman.

When she got back on the ferry itself she saw that the boy was swimming across the river after her. His dark face split in another grin and he popped a few more corks on the way. He came along quite quickly considering he used a queer sort of dog-paddle.

"There's nobody over here," Gilda shouted to her parents. They shrugged their shoulder and Mrs. Ronkoop went back to the car and sat in it.

The boy climbed up on the ferry. "Didn't you find that lazy ferryman yet?"

Gilda kept a dignified silence.

The boy had swum across in his shirt and shorts. He pressed them against his body to squeeze some of the water out and went to the cabin. A few seconds later Gilda heard the put-put of the engine. "Do you think you ought to play about in there?" she asked through the cabin door.

The boy merely grinned again and jerked a lever. The wheel began to turn slowly and the ferry to draw away from the bank.

Gilda was worried, expecting any moment to see an angry ferryman hopping about on the bank demanding the immediate return of his stolen ferry. When this did not happen it began to dawn on her that the boy was handling the machinery very efficiently. She went back to the cabin again.

"Why didn't you tell me instead of playing those stupid games?" she said sharply.

"Tell you what? What you mean, mate?" said the boy.

"Well, you *are* the ferryman, aren't you?"

The boy opened his eyes very wide. "Oh no," he said innocently. "That's my father.

He's the one gets paid for working the ferry." Then he put both hands over his mouth and ducked out of sight behind the wheel.

Oh well, thought Gilda, it was quite a good joke really, I suppose.

The Ronkoops' car was ferried across, and as they drove away Gilda saw the boy plunge back into the river. Why he should want to work the ferry from the wrong side of the water she could not imagine.

The Moogara Forest is a large one, broken into three sections by the wide bends in the river. The part of the forest the Ronkoops had now entered ran along the north bank of the Murray River for about fifty miles and was about twelve miles wide most of the way. As the river rose and flooded it at least once a year for a period of a couple of months, there were no proper roads, only hard dirt tracks which wound over the flat ground in and out of the mighty red gums.

Fortunately the main tracks were well marked with large blotches of red paint on the trunks of the gums on either side, and now and then when a track forked there was usually a rough board nailed to a tree trunk with an arrow and SAWMILLS painted on it. Following these indications, Mr. Ronkoop drove for nearly twenty miles into the forest. They passed a wide shallow lake with hundreds of black swans and pelicans swimming on it. Now and then they came on a small group of cattle that stared at them with dull expressions. Once half a dozen kangaroos fled from them, and once they passed an emu with two chicks, the chicks being about the size of hens.

Mr. Ronkoop began to get doubtful. He said, "Mr. Prentice said it was a good way from anywhere, but I didn't think it would be this far."

"Let us go back," said Mrs. Ronkoop. "It is no good."

"Oh no!" exclaimed Gilda. She found the forest weird and a little frightening, but at the same time there was something about it, a sort of secretive quiet, that made her feel they must go on. She tried to imagine what it would be like when the floods came, five or six feet up the tree trunks by the look of the dark marks on the rugged bark. "Oh please let's go on and *see!*" she urged.

Mr. Ronkoop said in a grumbling sort of way that having come so far they might as well, and drove on.

Only a few minutes after that they came to a bridge over a fair-sized creek fifteen or twenty feet wide and well filled with clear but greenish-colored water, and on the far side of the creek, built up on the bank, was a small wooden house labeled General Store and Post Office. Through the trees they caught glimpses of half a dozen other houses dotted about, mostly along the side of the creek.

"Well, here is somewhere," said Mr. Ronkoop, cheering up.

Mrs. Ronkoop refused to be cheered, however. "How somewhere?" she grumbled. "Here I still see nowhere. One house and you think we have a town, eh?"

It wasn't a town, of course, and the shop they had seen was the only one, but there were a few houses and even a school, very small but very modern with new paint and lots of glass. It looked as if it had been brought out on a truck and dropped down anywhere among the trees.

The road led as far as the sawmill and gave up even pretending to be a road anymore.

Being Sunday the sawmill was idle. The saws and the winches were still and no one moved among the piles of cut timber or the great rough tree trunks. A large gray and yellow bird watched them from the top of a baby mountain of bright red sawdust.

There was a neat house next to the mill; a house on stilts with enough room underneath for a car. High up on the veranda, protected from the sun by a bright green and white stripe awning, a man sat in a deck chair with a newspaper. He was not reading the paper; he was holding it in his lap and watching the Ronkoops. Mr. Ronkoop stopped the car and got out.

Gilda and her mother stayed in the car and about ten minutes later Mr. Ronkoop came back, slapping at the flies and giving them no hint from his expression as to what he was thinking.

"Well?" demanded Mrs. Ronkoop.

"The job seems to be all right. Good money anyhow. The manager told me where to find the house, so I reckon we'd better have a look at that before we make up our minds."

Gilda had already made up her mind. There was something about the Moogara Forest that she liked straight off, and she could not think of any other place they had been where she had felt this so strongly. She had her fingers crossed, hoping that the house would not be too bad, and that her mother could be persuaded to stay.

They went about a hundred yards beyond the sawmill and among the trees, but there was no sign of a house.

"That's odd," said Mr. Ronkoop. "The

manager said it was somewhere here. Another bridge over the creek, he said, and a small patch of fruit trees in the garden . . ."

"Well, there's the bridge," Gilda said, pointing to a broken-down mass of planks sinking into the soft mud of the creek bank. "And I expect that green patch is the garden . . ."

They walked toward the clump of trees which turned out to be a neat orchard with two peach trees, four apricots, four oranges, three pears and six fig trees. Weeds were waist deep among the trees, but the branches were well loaded with fruit.

Still no house.

They walked right around the orchard and then, with a sudden sinking in the heart, Gilda pointed and cried, "Do you think that's supposed to be the house?"

Mrs. Ronkoop gave one look and then groaned aloud. "Are you asking me to live in such a cowshed?" she demanded. "Sooner would I live forever in a good strong tent."

The School in the Forest

THE HOUSE was certainly in an awful state. To start with, it wasn't a very neatly designed house, but consisted of one very long barnlike shack, to which had later been added a second part, long, low and narrow, after the style of a railway carriage. The main part was built of slabs, the thick rough planks put edge to edge, and in fact letting a good deal of daylight through. The rusty iron sheets that had formed the roof were curled and bent, or slewed sideways, or in one or two cases simply were not there at all.

As to the second part or wing of the building, it was too squalid for words, with moldy rotten beams and tiny windows.

Well, Mr. Prentice had warned them, and now, here it was. Gilda waited, not at all certain of her own thoughts. The forest was beautiful, and to have a garden and orchard of their own was something she had hardly dared to dream about. But the house! Well, it certainly was like nothing she had ever drawn. All the same . . .

There was a long pause, during which Mr. Ronkoop walked up and down looking critically at the house, and Mrs. Ronkoop quite simply turned her back on it and went away to sit in the car.

"Um," Mr. Ronkoop was saying to himself. And then in Dutch as if speaking his thoughts aloud, "Only ten dollars a year. How can one lose? The fruit alone is worth more . . ."

Gilda knew from experience that it was her mother who usually had the last word, and there was her mother now sitting doggedly in the car and ready to move on.

She was all the more surprised therefore to hear her father say in a clear and definite voice, "We will unload the trailer and pitch the tent. I have told the manager I shall work for a month. During that time we will consider what can be done about the house."

"Here is no place for us," said Mrs. Ronkoop. "I can feel it is no good. We should move on now."

"I've given my word," said Mr. Ronkoop simply. "We shall stay. There is nothing more to discuss."

"A month!" cried Mrs. Ronkoop. "A whole month to live like savages in the wild woods!"

Mr. Ronkoop looked round. "I don't know," he said. "Already I feel it is a nice place. The quietness is so soft here."

"Nothing to see but trees and trees and more trees," said Mrs. Ronkoop. "Oh well, a month is only a month . . ." and she got out of the car and began to bustle around.

Very soon the tent was up, pitched at the side of the orchard in a spot from which the ramshackle house was out of sight, Gilda noticed. In less than an hour everything was neat and tidy with two stoves purring, the dinner bubbling in the saucepans and the table laid and ready.

Gilda finished her jobs first and went into the orchard to get some fresh fruit. The apricots were too ripe but would do for jam. The peaches and a few of the oranges were just right, so she gathered a dozen or so of each in her skirt and filled a bowl for the table.

It was amazing how quickly the Ronkoops settled down to their normal routine. The following morning Mr. Ronkoop went off to work at the sawmill, and at half past eight when Gilda went past on her way to school she stopped for a moment to listen to the changing song of the saw as it bit deeper into the red gum wood and to watch the cascade of bright sawdust pouring from the blower and adding more height to the sawdust mountain. She saw her father for a few minutes working the great winch that dragged whole trees up on to the sawing table; he was too busy to notice her, however.

Gilda wandered on along the creek, past the store which was just opening. Two children came out with bags of pretzels and stared at her curiously as she passed, but did not speak.

She walked right round the school, peeping in at the windows. It seemed to have only two classrooms, one with little tables and chairs for the infants, the other with desks. Everything was shining and new; she had never seen a school looking so smart and pretty before. And to make things even better there was a very pretty young teacher working at the teacher's desk. She had short fair hair and wore a gay summer frock as green and as yellow as a bunch of daffodils. Gilda wondered what color her eyes were.

She soon found out, for at that moment the teacher looked up and saw her. She immediately smiled, and jumping to her feet came to the door.

"Don't tell me you're a new student!" she said. Her eyes were blue with tiny pale flecks.

"We came yesterday," Gilda said.

"Well, isn't that exciting?" said the teacher. "We hardly ever get anybody new here. The children will be delighted. Now come in so that I can get all about you down in my book."

Gilda was quite bewildered by this reception. At every other school she had been to she had been treated as something of a nuisance. She stood by the table while the teacher took out a huge admission register and opened it up.

"Now then, name first!"

"Gilda Ronkoop."

Instead of writing it the teacher looked up and repeated it. "Gilda Ronkoop," she said, and then added in Dutch, "This gets better and better. First we have a new pupil, and then she turns out to be Dutch. My name is Van Heeumen. What do you think of that?"

"Are you Dutch too?" Gilda asked.

"Sort of. My parents came here ages ago. But I went to Holland for a while when I had finished at college."

Gilda said, "I don't speak Dutch very well. I'm always making silly mistakes."

"You speak it very nicely," said Miss Van Heeumen. "And I make mistakes too. But I love to speak it. We're very lucky to know how to speak two languages."

By and by the other children began to wander in and they were introduced to Gilda. She was surprised that they really did seem pleased to have her. A girl called Marion took her around and showed her where everything was, and another girl, a dark-skinned one with brown eyes and gentle hands, found her some reading books from the cupboard and lent her two new exercise books of her own.

The school was not run like any school Gilda had been in before. There were no bells or whistles, no standing in lines, and no cane. When Miss Van Heeumen said she thought it was time they started work, the children sat down at their desks and began. There was a great deal of laughing, and the children got up and wandered about the class-room getting things or helping each other almost as if they were at home. There were only ten children from eight to twelve in the class. The morning passed like a flash.

At dinnertime Gilda went back to the camp, and while she was eating she tried to tell her mother about how nice it was at school and how the teacher spoke Dutch.

"That is nice," said Mrs. Ronkoop. "We should ask her back one evening for tea perhaps. Only it is difficult when one lives in a tent."

"Maybe later," said Gilda. "When Dad has done something with the house."

"Oh, that house!" said Mrs. Ronkoop. "It is too bad. You can put that right out of your mind, I think."

At half past three when the children were going home Miss Van Heeumen called Gilda.

"Now," she said affably. "We must have a little talk."

Gilda thought she meant a talk in Dutch, but the teacher went on:

"You know you are very behind in your work, don't you?"

"Yes, Miss Van Heeumen. I think it is because we never stay in one place very long. And at most schools I just sit at the back of the class and no one pays much attention to me."

"Well, we can't have that, can we?" said Miss Van Heeumen. "How long are you going to be here?"

"I should like to stay," said Gilda. "But Mum doesn't seem to like it. But at least we shall be here for a month, because Dad told the manager at the mill he'd stay that long."

"A month!" said Miss Van Heeumen.

"That's a long time. We shall have you shooting ahead like a rocket, you see if we don't."

Gilda wasn't at all sure she wanted to shoot like a rocket which, as far as she knew, nearly always went off with a loud bang and shot colored stars all over the place. But she was happy that Miss Van Heeumen was pleased with her.

When Mr. Ronkoop came home from work he was pleased too." A very nice little job," he said, and repeated it two or three times during the evening. "Plenty to keep you busy so that the time doesn't drag, and everybody mighty friendly. In fact I have never been in so friendly a place."

"I tell you what I notice," said Mrs. Ronkoop. "No mosquitos. First place we have no mozzies for months, I reckon."

"It's a good place altogether," Mr. Ronkoop said. "You know, I think Rod would like to be here." Rod was Mr. Brunt's first name.

"Then you should write and tell him so," said Mrs. Ronkoop. "That would be nice for you, eh, Gilda?"

Gilda had not been listening; she had been thinking of her two new friends, and especially the aboriginal girl whose name was Carline and who had a deep, furry sort of voice. Carline had asked her to go to tea the next day after school. "What would be nice for me?" she asked.

"To have the Brunts here, of course," said her mother. "Your father just said he might write to them."

"Oh yes," said Gilda.

A few minutes later she wandered outside thinking to take a little stroll around the garden. The sun was just setting, however, so she sat by the creek for a while and then went over toward the broken-down house. For a minute or so she thought of the Brunts. She was not nearly so excited at the thought of them coming as she thought she would be. Perhaps it was because she seemed now to be doing something quite different from usual. Up till now she had always been rather a lonely girl. Suddenly she had two new friends, and everything around her seemed interesting and exciting. There did not seem time to look back.

She stood in front of the house and tried to imagine what it had looked like when it was new, but it was no use. The broken roof and the sour smell of rotten timber got in the way.

It was in a lovely spot, however, with the creek in front and those lovely fruit trees behind. The fig trees were even higher than the roof, holding their weird-shaped leaves like monstrous misshapen hands against the faintly pink sky.

She was about to turn away when she heard a scratching sound on the iron roof, then a rumbling noise as if someone was rolling a ball down. The thing hit the ground with a soft thud, bounced and rolled almost to her feet. It was a ripe peach. Gilda knew it must be a possum on the roof and that the creature must have been taking fruit from the orchard. She kept quite still and waited.

There was some more scratching and then a real thump as the possum dropped to the ground. She could just see it in the dark shadow at the foot of the wall. After a minute or so it began to come forward, a few steps at a time, testing each place on the earth before it put a paw down. A few steps, then a pause, then a few more steps.

When it reached the peach it gathered the fruit up between its forepaws, sat up and stared straight at Gilda. Neither of them moved. The possum had black ears and a black forehead, so that it seemed almost to have a mask on.

I don't mind you taking one or two peaches, Gilda thought. There are plenty there for everybody.

The possum might almost have read her

thoughts, for it held the fruit and began to eat it.

"I hope it's a nice ripe one," Gilda said quietly.

The possum shot up straight and stared at her with an amazed look. It had obviously mistaken her for a tree.

"I'm sorry," said Gilda. "I didn't mean to startle you."

This was more than the possum could bear. It dropped the peach and bolted for the nearest tree. There was a brief rattle of sharp claws on the trunk, then the creature reached the first branch and turned to make a noise like an angry steam engine at her. Gilda carried the peach over and put it at the foot of the tree.

Most of the aborigine families lived in small corrugated iron houses, which stood in a line on the bank of the creek just near the sawmill. These had been put up originally for workers at the mill until each family had built its own weatherboard house. They were very small, often only one room about ten feet square. Hardly houses at all, Gilda thought, having her own ideas about what a house ought to be like. But in fact the families using them spent most of their time outside and used the house as a bedroom.

When Carline and Gilda arrived from school next day Carline's mother was cooking over an open fireplace. She was a slim, pretty woman, very dark with black curly hair, and with gentle eyes of so dark a brown that they seemed almost black when the light was behind her. She smiled at Gilda and greeted her in the same husky sort of voice as Carline's.

"I've been wanting to see Carline's new friend," she said. "Such pretty hair you got."

Gilda suddenly felt nothing but contempt for her own wishy-washy blondness. "Oh this old stuff!" she said. "Be all right to fill a cushion with."

Carline's mother shook her head and smiled as if she knew better.

Suddenly they were surrounded by half a dozen smaller children, some of whom were Carline's brothers and sisters.

"You wanna see dead snake?" cried one.

"Look where dirty old lizard bit my leg!" said another, dancing on one foot as he held up the other for inspection.

"I catch you possum quick if you like," promised a small girl, a tiny bright-eyed child of five or six.

"Aren't they lovely?" Gilda said. "I wish I had lots of small brothers and sisters."

"They're all showing off," said Carline.

Then, turning to her mother, "How long till tea, Mum?"

"When your dad comes home. Half hour maybe. How about you and Gilda getting me some crayfish? They go nice with what I got here."

"Gilda won't want to catch any old crayfish," said Carline rather sulkily, as if ashamed of her mother for suggesting it.

"I like to," Gilda interrupted quickly. "It's good fun. I always used to go crayfishing with the Brunts."

"All right then," said Carline. "But not with all these kids."

The children protested loudly that they wanted to go crayfishing, and three or four clung tightly to Gilda's hands and stared up at her face with pleading expressions.

"Oh, let them come," she said, feeling their small warm fingers wriggling between her own. It was like having a whole handful of tiny, nuzzling, helpless, hairless puppies.

In the end they all went up the creek to a place where a fallen tree had made a natural dam and beyond which, in the deeper water, the crayfish were plentiful. There they all sat in a row on the log, dangling their black threads and raw meat into the water. They caught crayfish at a tremendous rate, little transparent ones and big black ones with fiercely snapping claws and tails as strong as clock springs. Carline's smallest sister, the one who had offered to catch Gilda a possum, caught the biggest crayfish Gilda had ever seen, and then got so excited about it that she dropped it back and tumbled into the water after it. She was rescued immediately, dragged out of the creek by her hair and one leg. She did not seem at all frightened. In fact she ran off to find her mother, shouting proudly, "That dirty old crayfish near ate me up! Mum! You hear me? That dirty old . . ."

There was a big savory dish of rice for tea, with all kinds of oddments of meat and fish and vegetables mixed in, and indeed the fresh crayfish did go very nicely with it. Gilda was pleasantly surprised when Carline's mother spread a cloth and laid out plates and knives and forks in a perfectly normal way.

"I read in a book," she said, "that you ate raw wichetty grubs and lizards and snakes and things like that."

Carline made a sound in her throat as if the idea revolted her, but her mother said, "My mother told me she used to eat wichetty grubs when she was little. But that was long time back, I reckon. Me now, I'd rather have fish and chips."

Carline's father had fixed up a very long swing from a high branch, and Carline and Gilda played on this for a while after tea. The swing went out over the creek, so that as you swung out on it you could look down between your knees and see the dark water beneath you, and this gave you a wonderful trembling feeling that if you didn't hold on tight you might fall all that way into the water.

"Come again," they said when Gilda decided it was time for her to go home. Then, as she and Carline went off along the bank, Gilda could hear the smaller children talking about her and saying, "She's real nice, that's what she is."

"They're just crazy kids," muttered Carline.

Gilda had a warm feeling inside. "I like them," she said. "I wish I could have them all for my brothers and sisters."

Carline went with her as far as the school, which was about halfway, then they separated and walked backward away from each other until Gilda stumbled over a root and sat down. Then they both laughed and turning around ran back toward their own homes.

"You seem very happy," said Mrs. Ronkoop when Gilda reached the camp. "You had a good time I think, yes?"

Water and Trees

Mr. Ronkoop wrote to the Brunts, but he heard nothing at all from them for a fortnight. Then a letter came from Mrs. Brunt saying that Mr. Brunt had been offered a permanent job at the factory and that they were thinking of renting a small house for a while.

"You see!" said Gilda. "Proper people live in houses."

"You and your houses," said Mrs. Ronkoop.

But Mr. Ronkoop smiled and gave Gilda a broad wink as if he had some sort of a secret which he might tell her about later.

Meanwhile two weeks at school had made a great deal of difference to Gilda. Miss Van Heeumen had been quite right. Gilda was improving in all her subjects, and so quickly that she half-suspected Miss Van Heeumen must have magical powers.

In fact, of course, the explanation was much simpler than that. Nowadays Gilda had so many friends at school that she preferred being there to being back at the camp. Her mother noticed this and asked her about it.

"School is more like a proper house," said Gilda. "Windows and doors and a proper floor — well, you see its different entirely from a tent."

"But you've been living in a tent for as long as you can remember," said her mother. "Why do you suddenly feel like this?"

"Oh, I don't know," said Gilda. "I just do."

Later that evening, when Gilda was strolling around the old house looking for her friendly possum, her father followed her.

"You know," he said, "I think I might be able to do something with that old place."

"If only you could," said Gilda.

"I mentioned it to the manager the other day," said Mr. Ronkoop. "He said I can take all the timber I want for nothing. It's only a question of the work."

Gilda said, "I'd help you if I'd be any use."

"You'd be a lot of use," said Mr. Ronkoop.

Later he spoke to his wife about it.

"That old house is past repair," she said

immediately. "You would just be wasting your time."

"Still, I might do a bit Saturdays and Sundays," Mr. Ronkoop said.

When Gilda mentioned this to Miss Van Heeumen the next day she said, "That old house? That's interesting. You know it was where Governor Brompton lived, don't you?"

Gilda had never heard of Governor Brompton.

"I've got a book I'll lend you," said Miss Van Heeumen. "It tells you about the first people who settled here in Moogara Forest. I think you'd like it."

She brought the book next day and Gilda took it home in the evening. She read the first three pages and was disappointed; it was like the dullest sort of geography lesson. However, she was flicking through the pages when she found a bookmark that Miss Van Heeumen had left between the pages, so she started reading again from where the marker was. This was about a man called Brompton who lived over a hundred years before. He had been looking for gold in one of the gold fields not far from Moogara, but had been unlucky. Then he overheard some of the miners saying they would pay any amount of money for the taste of some fresh fish.

Brompton gave up looking for gold and went north to the Murray River. There he caught fish and carried them back to the gold fields to sell to the miners. He made quite a lot of money this way. Then he discovered that he could sell fish to the captains of the river steamboats. He stopped making the long journey backwards and forwards between the river and the gold fields and settled down. He built himself a house by a creek in the Moogara Forest.

On the following page there was a picture of the house that Brompton built, not broken and dilapidated the way it was now, but smart and new, with a covered veranda. And a tower!

Gilda jumped up in her excitement.

"Dad!" she cried. "Just look at this!"

Mr. Ronkoop looked at the picture. "Well?" he said.

When Gilda explained that it was a drawing of their house the way it used to look, he became more interested and examined it closely.

"I could do this," he said. "It would be more interesting to make it as it used to be."

"With the tower?" asked Gilda.

Mr. Ronkoop looked doubtful. "What use is the tower?" he said. "You would not see over the trees surely."

"Perhaps there is something in the book about it," said Gilda and read further until she came to a part where the tower was mentioned. Apparently Brompton had built the tower so that he would have somewhere well above the flood level no matter how high the water rose. He even used to hang a lantern in the top of the tower so that people could find their way to his house, and he could find his own way home easily after a night's fishing.

"There you are," said Gilda.

"Maybe it is a good idea," said Mr. Ronkoop. "I don't know if I can do it. But I will see, and if a tower is possible, we will even have a tower."

After that Mr. Ronkoop would work for a while each weekend, sawing and banging over at the old house. Gilda went to help him sometimes, but as he was pulling down the old timbers and getting in a terrible mess with the dirt and dust, Mrs. Ronkoop put her foot down and said Gilda was to have nothing to do with the dirty business. Mrs. Ronkoop did not believe anything would come of her husband's efforts in any case, and she never tired of telling him that he was wasting his time.

Gilda spent more and more of her spare

time with her new friends, especially with Marion and Carline, either out of doors wandering in the forest, swimming in the river, or else being invited to their homes. On Saturdays or Sundays they often took a billy, a frying pan and some food and spent all day out, cooking their meals over a fire.

Gradually the summer passed and the winter came. The days were still warm, but the nights grew very cold. Mr. Ronkoop always had a big campfire blazing outside the tent, and Gilda would sit on a log by it while she did her homework. It did not rain very much in Moogara, but rain fell in the mountains far away to the east, and the river began to rise higher and higher up its banks. Eventually it began to overflow the banks and form irregular lakes in the forest.

"Whatever do you do when the whole forest is flooded?" Gilda asked Marion one day when the water had flowed over and covered one of their favorite hollows. "Will it flood the whole forest?"

"Sometimes it does," said Marion.

"What happens then? Does everybody stay at home all the time?"

"Of course not," Marion laughed. "We use our boats."

"You say that as if they were as common as bicycles."

"Well, so they are. If you look you'll see that everyone here has a boat tucked away under the house. It's quite fun really. Especially when strangers get lost in the forest and we have to go out and rescue them. When that happens at night all the boats have lights on them and it's like a carnival."

The floods kept on spreading and spreading as the weeks passed. Once the water had risen above the normal river banks, it went very quickly indeed over the flat country on either side. The creek in front of the Ronkoops' camp became a wide deep river. The mail, which all summer had been brought to the post office in a small red van, now came daily in a blue motorboat, which followed the twists and turns of the creek just as if it had been a regular roadway. The same boat brought meat and groceries and any other stores people might be wanting. And it always followed the creek, because although the water was often quite deep enough through the forest, there was always the danger of striking a submerged tree trunk or its branches hidden under the brown muddy waters.

Mr. Ronkoop found an old flat-bottomed boat of the sort used in the forest. It had been lying in the old house. He tried it on the creek and it let water in because it had dried out during the summer. A man at the sawmill told him to sink it in the creek for a few days.

"Once the wood has swelled with the water, she'll be right," he said.

It was good advice for after two or three days of soaking, the boat became quite watertight. Gilda practiced rowing all one weekend and was so pleased with herself that the following Monday she rowed to school, although this was not absolutely necessary as the school was on the same side of the creek as the Ronkoops' camp, and both were on the ridge of land that ran right through that part of the forest. But it was more fun than walking.

She called the boat *Sam Brompton* after the old man who had first lived in this spot and planted the trees in the orchard — or at least some of them; fig trees were said to live a very long time. She painted the letters in white on the bow. On the stern thwart she wrote "Prop: Gilda Ronkoop."

Everybody in the forest put his name on his boat like this, so that if a sudden rise of water carried a boat away it could be easily identified by the person finding it.

One evening about this time Gilda suddenly remembered that she had left the books she needed for homework on the bench in the school yard. As her father was not yet home from work and there was still at least half an hour before teatime, Gilda rowed up to the school in the *Sam Brompton*.

When she reached school the light was still on in the classroom and Miss Van Heeumen was working at her desk. Gilda found the books where she had left them, but went into the school to get a dictionary, which she did not really need but which might come in useful. Then she stayed to talk for a while with Miss Van Heeumen.

Almost the first thing Miss Van Heeumen said was, "I like the way your father is re-building the old Brompton house. You must have showed him that book I lent you."

"I did," said Gilda. "When he saw the picture he said it would be interesting to try and make it the way it used to be."

"That's just what he's done. Only he's improved on it," said Miss Van Heeumen. "I went for a walk round there the other evening. I had no idea he'd done so much to it."

Gilda had no idea either. She had not been round the other side of the orchard for two or three weeks. Now she felt rather guilty about it. After all, she had told her father she would help him, and apart from the first few times when she had got her clothes so dirty that Mrs. Ronkoop had been very cross, she had hardly been near the place. She must go and see as soon as she got home. Or at least first thing tomorrow morning.

"I suppose you'll be moving in fairly soon," said Miss Van Heeumen.

"Oh yes, I suppose so. Dad hasn't actually said . . ."

Mr. Ronkoop had not said a single word to anyone.

"I tell you what," said Miss Van Heeumen. "Once you move into that lovely house, you'll never want to leave the forest."

"I don't want to move anyway," said Gilda. "I never have. That's what's so queer about the forest. Although I'd never been here before, it was just like coming back to a place I knew well. Like coming home, I suppose, only I've never had a home."

Gilda would have liked to ask the teacher if the new house had a tower like the one in the picture, but she couldn't very well. After a while she said she thought she ought to be getting back to her tea, and Miss Van Heeumen said she still had a great deal of work to do. So a little later still Gilda left.

By this time it was quite dark. Gilda climbed into the *Sam Brompton* and rowed slowly back toward the camp. She rowed slowly because she was thinking how nice Miss Van Heeumen had been, and how pretty she was, and how you didn't often get a teacher who was nice and also really pretty the way Miss Van Heeumen was.

After about ten minutes, or it might have been longer, she thought to herself she ought to be about level with the tent by now and looked around for the light. This was usually easy to find because the canvas of the tent was green, making the light green when it shone through.

Not only could she not see a green light, but she could not see any light at all, except of course from the stars, which were not much help.

"This is ridiculous," she said aloud, "I've only been rowing a few minutes. Perhaps Miss Van Heeumen has put the school light out and I haven't gone quite far enough to see the tent yet."

She rowed a little farther, glancing over her shoulder all the time, waiting for the green light to appear.

Then she noticed she had somehow or other got among the trees. Usually when she rowed from camp to school, she kept out of the creek itself because of the current and rowed in the open water just over the other side. But there were no trees for about a hundred yards as they had all been cleared away in the past.

She pulled on one oar to turn in what she judged to be the direction of the creek, but the trees were still there; in fact she had to turn and twist to avoid bumping into them, and this is rather difficult when you are rowing and looking over your shoulder the whole time.

"Oh dear," she said at least, still speaking aloud because the sound of her own voice comforted her, "I shall have to turn around and go back. Then I can start again."

Turning a boat, in the dark, to go back the way you've come, is not particularly easy. Gilda turned until she thought she must be pointing in the opposite direction and then rowed, hoping to see the outline of the school building against the lighter background of the sky. No school appeared. All the time she rowed she was surrounded by water and trees, and the trees in the dark all look very much alike.

A quarter of an hour later Gilda shipped her oars and began to cry quietly to herself. There was no longer any doubt about it; she was lost in the Moogara Forest.

Stars Are Useless

WHEN Gilda did not return immediately with her books, Mrs. Ronkoop thought she had probably called in at the sawmills on the way back and would be coming when her father stopped work. Time passed, however, the tea was cooked and ready, and still no one came. Mrs. Ronkoop began to wonder what had happened.

She walked down to the school and found it dark and deserted, and then went to the sawmill, which was also quiet with only one light on a pole in the middle of the wood yard, giving the red stacks of cut timber a ghostly orange appearance.

The mill manager was surprised when Mrs. Ronkoop asked about her husband. "He hasn't been in to work at all today," he said. "Or yesterday either, for that matter. I gave him a couple of days off because there were some jobs he wanted to get finished."

"Jobs?" asked Mrs. Ronkoop. "What jobs?"

The manager smiled. "I reckon you'll find that out pretty soon," he said.

"Anyway, if Gilda is with him I don't need to worry," said Mrs. Ronkoop.

But when she got back to the camp Mr. Ronkoop was there alone, lifting lids off saucepans, sniffing and looking hungry.

"Where is everybody?" he exclaimed. "I nearly made a start, I am so hungry."

When Mrs. Ronkoop told him about Gilda taking the boat to school and not coming back, he forgot about being hungry. He said he would go and borrow the mill manager's motorboat and look for Gilda in the forest.

Mrs. Ronkoop said, "I saw the manager and he said you'd not been working since two days."

"Working?" said Mr. Ronkoop. "I've been working all right. But I'll tell you about it later when I've found Gilda. You stay here and keep the food warm. And don't worry."

"How can I not worry, eh?" said Mrs. Ronkoop. "Just tell me that, eh?"

Out in the forest in the *Sam Brompton* Gilda had stopped crying and was trying to be sensible. She talked aloud to herself.

"If you know anything about the stars,"

she said, "you can find your way quite easily. So it just serves you right for not knowing enough. I bet Carline knows all about the stars. I bet anything you like she simply never gets lost."

She peered up among the branches at the sky and at all its millions of stars and felt quite dizzy. Somehow or other among all that glitter was the Southern Cross, which would tell her where the south was, and from it she ought to be able to get her direction.

"The trouble is," she said, speaking to the stars this time, "you're all so untidy. You're worse than trees. If only you were in nice neat rows . . . or if you had names printed on you like streets . . ."

Then, low down in the sky, she found some stars that she thought must be the Southern Cross, because they made the same shape — rather like a kite — as the stars on the Australian flag.

"Well," she exclaimed, giving her neck a rub because it had got stiff with so much looking upward, "that's a start. So the south is over there. Now the question is, which way do *I* want to go?"

And this, she suddenly realized, was much more difficult, as she had no idea which way she had already gone.

"Oh!" she exclaimed to the Southern Cross, "you're no use at all. I can't think what makes people say you can find your way by the stars! When you're really lost, stars are nothing but a waste of time."

A little later she remembered that the tracks in the forest were marked by splashes of red paint on certain trees. If she had had a torch she could have looked for trees with paint on, and by following them would in the end come to a signboard which would tell her which way to go. Unfortunately the red paint was not the sort that shows up in the dark, and she had no torch. However, it was no use sitting and doing nothing, so Gilda rowed herself over to the nearest tree and felt the bark with her hand.

"If you've got a patch of paint on you," she said, "I shall feel it smooth and shiny."

She tried half a dozen trees like this without success, and began to realize that it would take her hours perhaps to find just one tree.

"I might just as well lie down in the bottom of the boat and sleep," she said. "In the morning, when I can see, it will be much easier."

It did occur to her that if the boat was caught by a current it might be carried down to the river and then on for miles without her knowing anything about it, so she tied the painter to a small tree and shipped her oars again.

"There!" she exclaimed. "Now nothing really bad can happen to me. In fact, if I had a blanket it would be quite fun. Of course, I can't very well do my homework, but I've certainly got a very good excuse."

Then she imagined Miss Van Heeumen asking her about it the following day.

"I'm very sorry, Miss Van Heeumen," Gilda answered in her politest school voice, "but I was adrift in an open boat all night."

"That's all very well," said Miss Van Heeumen, "but you should have done your homework *first*."

While she had been having this imaginary conversation, Gilda had been trying to get comfortable in the bottom of the boat. She now found that this was not possible, as there were a couple of inches of water slopping about on the boards. She had nothing to bale it out with, and the thought of sitting all night with her feet in water made her feel suddenly quite miserable.

For some time after that Gilda sat with her feet up on the thwart and her knees hugged to her chest. She began to feel chilly; not that it was very cold. The stillness and the loneliness made it seem much colder than

118

it was. She began to listen to the night noises of the forest, noises that had not worried her when she was busy trying to find her way, but which now began to sound eerie.

Some of these noises she recognized; the sad cry of the little boobook owl, the frogs which made noises like castanets and bongo drums, and the scratching of the possums as they made their slow and cautious way along the branches overhead. Beyond all this, however, there was a sound she could not identify; a sort of hollow gobble-gobble-gobble, sometimes interrupted by a high twanging sound. At first it was so distant that the slightest movement of the air carried it away, but every now and again she heard it and wondered.

Five or ten minutes later Gilda suddenly realized that the sound was much louder. It was still quite a long way off, but now it was echoed faintly by water and trees, so that it seemed to come from all directions at once. It was not a sound any animal she knew could make. It was certainly coming closer.

Gilda was not a superstitious girl, but now she began to recall some of the stories that Carline had told her about the forest. Carline said that sometimes floating tree trunks, glowing with green light and moving against the current as if with a life of their own, were to be seen in the forest. Red gum is a heavy wood and will not float in water; these floating, gleaming tree trunks were a mystery.

Carline also told tales of strange fearsome creatures that had never been seen by daylight and were not shaped like any ordinary animal. They were said to lie among the boughs of trees in the Moogara Forest and hang down their arms, on which were curved claws sharper than fish hooks.

"I don't believe a single word of it," cried Gilda aloud, defying the noisy darkness.

"Gobble-gobble-pangy-twangy," came the strange noise. It was not very far off now.

Gilda pulled on the painter so that the little *Sam Brompton* went in very close to the tree. She put out a hand and felt the thin crackly bark and it comforted her a little.

"Olly-bomp-baysie," came the sound. It was as if some creature, almost human, was trying to imitate ordinary speech.

Gilda strained her eyes in the direction from which the sound seemed to be coming, and then clung more tightly to the tree. About a hundred yards away, moving silently in and out among the trees, came something that glowed faintly green. It was long, like a tree trunk. Gilda began to shiver.

She could not remember what Carline had said about the green-glowing tree, but she thought she had said something about it being very bad luck to look at it. Gilda drew right back behind her tree, hoping that whatever it was it would float past without molesting her.

After a few seconds, though, she felt she could bear the suspense no longer. Whatever it was it made no sound now, and she imagined it must be approaching her from the blind side, that it must be almost on her. She peeped quickly. The green light was brighter, and in the very centre of the light she could make out a faint misty shape, a little like a human face but green, with black holes for eyes and nostrils and no top to the head at all. She could not stop herself letting out a sort of choked scream.

There was an immediate splash.

Then a deep voice said, "Man! That owl gave me a real scare. Now I've lost my flaming oar!"

Gilda took a deep breath and let it out again; she did not seem to have been breathing at all for ages.

"Who is it?" she called in a papery voice.

"Francis Hagan," answered the deep voice immediately. "Who are you?"

Francis Hagan was the name of Carline's

uncle, who was in fact the ferryman back at the river.

"Gilda Ronkoop!" cried Gilda quickly, untying her boat and pulling over in the direction of the other. It was easy to see now that the glow was simply the light from a small latern set on the floorboards, shining up at Hagan and his passenger.

"Carline," exclaimed Gilda. "I was just thinking of you. I was remembering the stories you told me about the tree trunks that glowed green . . ."

"Don't, please," cried Carline. "I've been trying to forget them all this time. Uncle lost his way and I was frightened we should be spending all night out in the forest. It's a good thing we ran into you . . ."

"I'm lost too," said Gilda. "I can't help you much."

"Well," said Carline, looking on the bright side, "we can't be quite so lost as we were if there are more of us."

Hagan said, "I'm not lost at all. I keep telling you. All that's wrong is I don't seem to be able to find the way."

When the two girls laughed at this he rumbled, "That's not a joke. Like I keeping telling you, in the old days in my father's time, there used to be a light hung up in Sam Brompton's tower. Then people could look up and see it and know where to go."

"What help's that?" said Carline. "There's no light in Sam Brompton's tower now, is there? Not even a tower for anyone to put a light in."

"I was saying what happened in the old days," began Hagan, and then suddenly broke off and stared.

Gilda followed his gaze and saw that a light was shining some distance away, and high up in the trees.

"That's where she always used to shine," said Hagan, and began to row again.

"But it can't possibly be the proper light," objected Carline. "Sam Brompton's tower's gone. It may be a sort of ghost light."

Hagan paused in his rowing for a second. "Ghost light?" he said. Then he shook his head. "I don't care what sort of light it is; it's where old Sam's light used to be and that's good enough for me."

They had been rowing toward the light for ten minutes or so when they heard the sound of a motorboat and saw the boat's light sweeping brokenly through the trees. When all three of them shouted together the light turned toward them and the boat began to chug over in their direction. A few minutes later Mr. Ronkoop's voice came over the water. "Is that you, Gilda?"

Such Crazy

IT WAS Miss Van Heeumen who had the idea about putting the light in the tower that Mr. Ronkoop had just finished building. Only Miss Van Heeumen could have thought of it, for she was the only one of the few people that knew what Mr. Ronkoop was doing who also knew the story of old Governor Brompton and his lamp.

That evening, after Gilda had been speaking to her at the school, and in fact while Gilda was getting herself lost in her boat, Miss Van Heeumen had strolled round to the new house to have another look at it. On the way back in the dark she had met Mr. Ronkoop just after he had borrowed the motorboat from the mill manager. At first she was going to jump in the boat with him to help look for Gilda. Then she changed her mind.

"No, you go on, Mr. Ronkoop," she said.

"I'll find a lantern and get it fixed up in that tower of yours. It's what old Brompton used to do to help people who were lost."

"That's a good idea," said Mr. Ronkoop. "I'll keep my eye open for it. Just like our own lighthouse, eh?"

So he went off to find Gilda, while Miss Van Heeumen put a lantern in the tower.

The house by this time was almost finished. Mr. Ronkoop had been doing extra work on it in order to get it ready for Gilda's birthday, as a surprise. Gilda's birthday was not, in fact, for another week. Of course after the rescue there could be no more question of a surprise. The very next morning as soon as it was light, Gilda got up and ran round the other side of the orchard to see both the new house and the tower.

Mr. Ronkoop had indeed made a beautiful job of it. He had copied the picture as far as the general shape of the house was concerned, making the tower and the covered veranda exactly as they used to be. As to the house itself, he had made it quite a lot larger and put in much bigger windows to catch the sunshine. He had also laid tiles, pale blue like clear sea water, to make a terrace in front of the house.

While Gilda was looking at the house, a large motorboat came chugging up the creek and a man shouted to her, asking where he would find Mr. Ronkoop. Gilda fled. She was still only in her nightie. She told her father though, and he said:

"Right, I will go and see what he wants, but no one is to come until I tell them. No one."

So Mrs. Ronkoop and Gilda had their breakfast and waited, wondering what all the excitement was about, but not even peeping to find out.

"He is a good man, your father," said Mrs. Ronkoop. "Who else would make a house out of such a pigsty? Didn't I tell you he would make a fine work of it?"

Gilda could only remember her mother saying it would be a waste of time, but she thought this was not the moment to start an argument.

Just before midday, Mr. Ronkoop came back to the camp looking rather hot and untidy, as if he had been carrying heavy weights about. "All right," he said. "You can both come and look now. This is really your birthday surprise, Gilda, but I don't suppose you will want to wait another week."

When they stood in front of the house and had told Mr. Ronkoop how lovely it looked, he said, "You must understand it is not completely ready yet. But some of it is. Enough to move in if you would like to."

"Move in?" cried Mrs. Ronkoop. "A house with no furniture?"

"Come and see," he said.

They followed him through the front door into a pleasant sunny hallway, then through into the living room. It was completely furnished, even to curtains and a beautiful green wall-to-wall carpet. Beyond that was the kitchen with a new electric stove, a refrigerator and gleaming surfaces and cupboards everywhere. Mrs. Ronkoop was almost speechless for once. Then she said, "But the money for all this? Where did the money come from?"

"The money I had saved for a house," said Mr. Ronkoop. "The house has cost me nothing but hard work and a little for nails and hinges and glass. So I spent what I had saved on furniture instead."

Gilda was dying to ask about the tower and when that would be finished. But, after all, if her father had done two rooms she could hardly expect . . .

"Why don't you run up and see your little room?" said her father. "Of course, it is not quite . . ."

Gilda did not wait to hear the rest, but she ran through the hall and under the arched doorway she had already noticed and guessed led up to the tower.

A wooden staircase spiraled up into the tower, making one complete turn before coming up through a hole in the floor into the room at the top. Gilda stopped on the top step and held her breath in case it wasn't real. The room was finished. A new bed, a dressing table, work table and chair, and a triangular-shaped cupboard that fitted into a corner. The door of the cupboard was open and on the shelves were all her private possessions from her old fruit box, which Mr. Ronkoop must have smuggled up here without her knowing.

A narrow balcony ran right round the outside of the four windows that faced north, south, east, and west out over the forest.

"It is for you and Sam Brompton," said her father from the stairs.

"It's the nicest present we ever had," said Gilda. "Can I ask Miss Van Heeumen to tea now?"

"Of course," said Mrs. Ronkoop. "With that beautiful kitchen to make cakes and jellies and pies in . . . we could have a party every night."

"Every night," cried Mr. Ronkoop, holding his hand on his forehead. "Listen to her? Such crazy!"